DETROIT PUBLIC LIBRARY

3 5674 04717424 9

KNAPP BRANCH LIBRARY
13330 CONANT
DETROIT, MI 48212
852-4283

D0880144

DEC 08

KN

KNAPP BRANCH LIBRARY
13330 CONANT
DETROIT, MI 48212
852-4283

OFFICE POLICY

SOME RULES ARE MEANT TO BE BROKEN

A.C. ARTHUR

Genesis Press, Inc.

Indigo Love Stories

An imprint of Genesis Press, Inc.
Publishing Company

Genesis Press, Inc.
P.O. Box 101
Columbus, MS 39703

All rights reserved. Except for use in any review, the reproduction or utilization of this work in whole or in part in any form by any electronic, mechanical, or other means, not known or hereafter invented, including xerography, photocopying and recording, or in any information storage or retrieval system, is forbidden without written permission of the publisher, Genesis Press, Inc. For information write Genesis Press, Inc., P.O. Box 101, Columbus, MS 39703.

All characters in this book have no existence outside the imagination of the author and have no relation whatsoever to anyone bearing the same name or names. They are not even distantly inspired by any individual known or unknown to the author and all incidents are pure invention.

Copyright© 2004, 2008 by A.C. Arthur. All rights reserved.

ISBN-13: 978-1-58571-281-6
ISBN-10: 1-58571-281-7
Manufactured in the United States of America

First Edition 2004
Second Edition 2008

Visit us at www.genesis-press.com or call at 1-888-Indigo-1

DEDICATION

To D-Trim…thanks for always having my back!

PROLOGUE

Staff meeting.

A roomful of attorneys had assembled around the long conference room table to review caseloads and settlement options. Charles Benton was at the head of the table, along with one of the partners, Byran King, who, after thirty-two years of practicing law, rarely did anything now but show up for staff meetings.

Keith sat directly across from Cienna watching her every move—how her head tilted to the side as she listened to whoever was speaking at the time and the way her eyes remained fixed on the person to whom she was speaking, the way she held her pencil between long, slender fingers with nails polished and perfectly manicured. He could almost feel those nails raking over the skin of his back as he pumped mercilessly into her. Whenever she spoke, her melodious voice ignited a fire deep within him.

He'd been watching her like this for about a month now. Ever since Chris had pointed out that if he weren't married, he'd be sweating her like a horny teenager. Keith knew the guy was full of hot air, and he'd seen firsthand how Cienna had brushed him off along with all the other attorneys in the office, and the remark had brought his attention to her once again. He'd forgotten about her for a while and explored other options but now he was back to her.

Mmmmmm. He watched her lick her lips. Damn, what he wouldn't do to have her licking him like that. Placing his hand between his legs he quickly adjusted his growing erection. He didn't think she even knew what she did to men.

"So, Keith, do you have anything to say?" Charles asked. "Keith?" he asked again.

Clearing his throat, Keith shifted in his chair and returned his hands to the table. "Oh, I'm sorry, Charles. No. I think that's it." He hoped that was the correct answer, considering he hadn't been paying a bit of attention to the meeting agenda.

"Okay, meeting adjourned," Charles announced. People began to collect their legal pads and pens and file out of the conference room. As Cienna rose from her seat, his eyes were riveted to her breasts; her nipples puckered through the sheer material of her blouse. *Was she aroused? Did she know what he had been thinking about her?*

Cienna had been sitting across the table from Keith trying like hell to think of anything but him. He hadn't talked much in today's meeting, instead just sat there looking as fine as ever. He'd left his jacket in his office, and his muscles strained against his cotton dress shirt. With each breath he took, the rise and fall of his chest caused her mouth to water. She yearned to kiss every ebony inch of him.

She'd tried not to be attracted to him. Lord knows, she didn't want to want him, but damned if she could control her craving for him. Every time she saw him—every time she heard his voice—her heart did somersaults, and her juices began to flow.

Now, he was quietly sitting there deep in thought. She wished they were alone in that room, wished he would put those big thick hands on her, wished he'd caress her breasts and take them into his mouth. *Oooooh*, his mouth, God, she'd love to feel that on her too.

But alas, he was a co-worker, which, one way or another, always spelled trouble. Her desire had to be suppressed. It was inappropriate and unprofessional, as she had learned from prior experience. She reminded herself of that as she stood to leave and didn't even look in his direction. Instead, she hurried out of the room as if the devil himself were chasing her.

CHAPTER ONE

Nine months later.

"Good morning, Benton and King," Reka cheerfully spoke into the phone. "No, I'm sorry, Mr. Page isn't in the office yet this morning. Would you like his voicemail?" Her fingers were already poised to push the appropriate button to transfer the call.

"No, ma'am, I cannot take your message. It is our policy to use the voicemail system." The woman on the phone was beginning to irritate her. "I can assure you that at some point in the near future, Mr. Page will check his voicemail for messages." The woman still didn't get it. She apparently wanted Reka to track the man down and give him the message personally, but that was not her job. Even if he were in, she wasn't about to get up from her desk to take him or anybody else a message.

"Ma'am, I can put you into his voicemail or you can call back later." Reka's voice strained with annoyance. "Well, I'm sorry if you don't like the voicemail system, but that's the way our office functions. Please feel free to call Mr. Page later." Pressing the appropriate button, Reka disconnected the call and rolled her eyes.

"Silly ass woman," she muttered to herself—at least she thought it was to herself before she looked up to see Tacoma getting off the elevator.

"Who was that? One of Keith's ladies?" he asked as he hung his suede jacket in the closet and proceeded to brush the invisible lint off his tight black sweater.

"Yeah, he probably took her to a nice, expensive restaurant for dinner then back to her place, sexed her like crazy until they fell asleep, and she's just now rolled over to cuddle with him only to find he's up and gone," Reka surmised. She smiled to herself, thinking how she'd love to be sexed like crazy by Keith Page.

"Child, you know that's right," Tacoma chirped. His hand lingered a little longer on a non-existent piece of something he was trying to remove from his sweater. Then his eyes seemed to glaze over, and his tongue moved slowly across his top lip. "Oooh, what I wouldn't do to roll over next to that man," Tacoma crooned in a sultry voice.

"Yeah, right. You'll be in line right behind me." Reka's voice was like cold water splashing over his head. "You know Keith doesn't swing that way."

"You never know. A big strong man like Keith? He might be something else behind closed doors." Just as he finished his remarks the elevator bell rang, signaling a new arrival.

"Good morning," Tyrese spoke, breezing in from the elevator. She walked over to the time clock to punch herself in. "Who are y'all up here talking about this early in the morning?" she asked the two who had mysteriously stopped talking when she walked in.

"Oh, nobody. How was your weekend, dear?" Tacoma asked her.

Reka rolled her eyes; she hated to hear about Tyrese's weekends. They were always so glamorous, so exciting, and so full of it she could puke.

"Oh, we didn't do much. We went out to the house. You know, they have the frame up now, and we took some pictures. I'll show them to you later. I've got to put this case down. It's killing my back." She fiddled with the Coach briefcase she carried.

Reka wondered why she even bothered to carry it, like she was that important. She was only the book-keeper; she didn't have anything in that bag that had jack to do with the firm. "You took pictures of wood again?" Reka asked, not making any attempt to hide her disgust.

"It's not just wood; it's my house. Come around to my office, and I'll show you." Speaking specifically to Tacoma, she cast Reka a hateful look. She knew Reka couldn't move from the front desk, which was the plan, as she didn't want to show them to her anyway.

Reka was just jealous because she lived in a little apartment in the city.

"I'll be right around," Tacoma promised as Tyrese turned the corner to her office. "Like I wanna look at some wood in the middle of a forest," he added to Reka.

"Well, you should have told her that." Reka rolled her eyes. She hated phony people, and while Tacoma was a good friend, at times he could be as phony as a two-dollar bill.

Cienna Turner stepped off the elevator and walked to the closet to hang up her coat. Reka was on the phone with one of her boyfriends (she was sure), so she didn't bother stopping to speak. Before she could reach her office, Max, one of the firm's partners stopped her.

"Hey, Cienna," he spoke with a bright smile.

"Hi, Max," Cienna greeted him. When she tried to walk around him to her office, he just stepped to the side with her.

"I was wondering if maybe you'd like to get some dinner tonight," he said. Maxwell Jones was in his early forties and had been at the firm for about twenty years. He did good work, and Cienna respected him for that. His wife had divorced him last year after he'd returned from Aruba with his personal trainer. Ever since then, he'd been on the prowl. This was the fourth time in the last six months that he'd asked her out.

"No, Max, I don't think that's a good idea. Besides, I already have plans for tonight," she said casually. She was used to his advances, along with the ones from some of the other attorneys in the office.

"Come on, it'll be fun. It's about time we got to know each other better." He casually placed a hand on her shoulder.

"No, I think we know each other only as well as colleagues should. Now, if you'll excuse me, I have work to do." She tried stepping to the side once more. This time, when he moved to step with her, she frowned and lightly pushed him aside and proceeded into her office.

"Well, your loss." Hunching his shoulders, he walked away.

"Yeah, I'm sure," she muttered to herself. As she dropped her briefcase on the floor behind her desk, she briefly wondered why it was that every man she met thought he had to hit on her.

It had been that way all of her adult life and most of her childhood. Even as a child, she'd drawn attention. She had been an exceptionally pretty baby, and her parents had snapped every picture of her they could. They were so proud of their daughter's beauty they'd invested a fortune in Kodak.

In high school, the boys had been drawn to Cienna—the football team, the baseball team, the debate club, everyone. Even the male teachers had always been just a tad too friendly with her, always asking her to stay after class so they could go over the lessons with her. Cienna hadn't had a problem with any of her schoolwork, so at first the requests for her to stay behind to receive extra tutoring were a bit baffling. But when the sessions began to focus more on her and what she was doing in her personal life than on English or math, Cienna knew something was wrong.

She'd been forced to learn early in life how to brush men off; she was convinced that they saw only her exterior attributes. They didn't know what was inside, nor did they seem to care.

Her senior prom date, Darryl Simpson, had been the captain of the football team. Darryl was gorgeous in his own right, so of course only the prettiest girl in school would do for him. Their pictures were, of course, dazzling. Everyone wanted to be them. They had been voted most likely to succeed and best-looking couple.

This had pleased Darryl to no end, but Cienna had remained unmoved by the ridiculous awards and the unwanted attention they seemed to bring to her.

Once in college, Cienna had foolishly thought that she'd meet more mature men, with goals and aspirations. But once again, the best-looking males who had nothing on their mind besides her looks had confronted her. They didn't care that she was a straight-A student. They didn't care what she intended to do with her degree in criminal justice. They only cared about how her hair was fixed and what she was wearing on their date that night.

Cienna had long since given up shallow partnerships with men. She'd resigned herself to being alone. While she occasionally dated and sometimes went so far as to sleep with a few of her dates, in the end they always came up short.

She wondered now, years later, if she'd always be alone. It hadn't bothered her so much in the past, but she was twenty-nine now and her biological clock was ticking. Still, she was bombarded with men of no substance, men of no character and men of no sense. Bobby had been a perfect example of this, a mistake which she had no intention of repeating. Refusing to open that door, she shook her head vehemently.

So if that meant she'd be alone, then so be it. She'd have her career, and that would have to be enough.

Rubbing her eyes, she allowed herself a few minutes to regroup after that trip down memory lane. When she opened them again and refocused on where she was and what she was supposed to be doing, she noticed there were two files on her chair (probably new cases), message light was flashing on her phone and there was a bright yellow sticky note on her computer screen that read, "Cienna, see me in my office at 10:30. Charles."

That was just what she needed first thing on a Monday morning—a meeting with the boss. The phone on her desk buzzed just before Reka's voice filled the room via intercom.

"Hey, girl, I was talking to that damn Jeff, so I couldn't say good morning," she rattled.

"Good morning, Reka." Cienna turned her computer on.

"Girl, you ain't gonna believe what he did this time. He had the nerve to come up in the bar with some silly-looking chick, tryin' to tell me she's his brother's girl. What's he think I am, a cabbage head? Uh, wait a minute; I'll call you back. I gotta get the phone."

Cienna shook her head and laughed to herself. Reka and her soap opera life. Every day she had a story because something was always wrong with somebody she knew. A few seconds later, Tacoma came into her office. Now here was another one with something always going on.

Tacoma was as gay as they come, but as sweet as cherry pie. He was, as always, impeccably dressed. Small framed, his hair was cut and trimmed and dyed a golden blonde that wasn't too offensive and seemed to fit him perfectly.

"Hey, Cee Cee, what's shakin'?" he asked. He proceeded to shake his ass into the chair on the other side of Cienna's desk.

"Good morning, Tacoma. How was your weekend?" She dreaded what was sure to be a detailed answer.

"Well, I went shopping. I told Terry, 'Look, I need some new clothes.' You know, we're going to Cancun next month. So I need some tank tops and things like that," he continued.

"Don't forget your Speedo." Cienna couldn't resist. Tacoma and his partner were both in their mid-forties and trying desperately to fight the aging process. So the mere thought of the two of them running along the beaches of Cancun in Speedos was hilarious to her.

"Now, you know I ain't puttin' on no Speedo for nobody. I'm a little too old for that. But I did find these nice swim trunks with parrots on them. They're green and blue and yellow. Doesn't that sound cute?" he asked.

"They sound...interesting," Cienna answered.

Reka buzzed in again. "So let me finish telling you," Reka started, not caring that Cienna hadn't picked up the receiver so that her voice could be heard throughout Cienna's office.

"Excuse me, miss, I was tellin' her about *my* weekend, thank you," Tacoma interrupted.

"Tacoma, you need to be getting to that copy job. Besides, we've all heard about your shopping spree and how Terry's going to kill you for spending so much money. We don't need to hear it again," Reka answered.

"Well, we've all heard about your cheatin'-ass boyfriend, and we don't need to hear that again," Tacoma retorted.

Finally reaching her limit with both of their drama-filled lives, Cienna interrupted their conversation. "Can you two take this out of my office? I have work to do." This happened every day. Every day, Tacoma was in and out of her office, gossiping, slacking off, talking—whatever you might want to call it, he was doing it. And Reka called her a million times a day to say nothing. It was a wonder Cienna ever got anything done.

CHAPTER TWO

"Good morning, Charles, you wanted to see me?" Cienna stuck her head into Charles Benton's office. Charles sat behind a huge oak desk in a large leather chair that seemed to swallow his small frame. He wore thick brown-rimmed glasses and talked with a lisp.

"Good morning, Cienna. It's nice to see you. Come, come, take a seat." Charles pointed to the chair closest to his desk. Cienna opted for the one farthest away, as Charles tended to have a juicy mouth and the more he talked, the more you were likely to get showered with spittle.

"What's going on?" she asked. She wanted to get this meeting over with. She had never liked the way Charles looked at her, although it was sometimes hard to tell if he was really looking at her at all because of the thick lenses he wore.

"I'll get to that in just a second. I'm waiting for someone else to join us." At that exact moment, his office door swung open again, and Keith Page came strolling in.

"Charles, you wanted to see me?" he asked. He took a seat and turned toward Cienna, as if he'd just noticed her. "Good morning, Cienna." Truth be told, he'd smelled her soft floral scent the minute he'd entered. It intoxicated his senses.

Keith had always prided himself on having self-control, meaning he didn't drool over a gorgeous woman when he saw one. But Cienna Turner was an exception. Hard as he tried, he couldn't help being mesmerized by her beauty.

He wasn't a bad-looking guy himself and he knew the ladies liked him well enough. So having a good-looking woman on his arm any given night of the week wasn't foreign to him. But Cienna was different. She didn't allow her beauty to overwhelm her. She was smart and an excellent attorney. That only added to the attraction. Beauty and brains were the perfect package to him.

"Good morning, Keith," she said, trying not to stare too long. Keith Page was Benton and King's hottest commodity, in more ways than one. He was an excellent litigator and was bringing the firm bundles of money, but besides that, he was damn good-looking. Six-foot-five, with broad shoulders, skin the color of a cold root beer, and a voice that was topped only by Billy Dee Williams, Keith definitely had it going on. But Cienna kept all those opinions to herself.

"Yes, I called the two of you here because I have something for you." Charles hesitated, looking from one attorney to the other. "Cienna, you've been doing an excellent job defending the city in that class action suit. I hear it's very near settlement."

"Actually it settled late Friday. One million even," Cienna said proudly. She had celebrated her latest victory all weekend.

"That's perfect. It would have been horrific had it gone to trial," Charles added.

"I know. The workers had a pretty good case. Too bad they couldn't afford to pay an expert to back them up."

"Yeah, that's just too damn bad," Charles said with a smirk on his face. "And Keith, you managed to keep the police department from losing a pretty penny, too."

"That was one hell of a trial, Charles. I don't know how we won it, but we did," Keith said, giving Cienna a cocky grin.

"We won because we had the better attorney, and he had a loaded gun. That's how we did it," Charles said. "Anyway, enough stroking your egos. We have a new case that just came in over the weekend. An old college friend of mine has gotten himself into a bit of trouble. You may have heard of him, as he's been in the news a lot lately, Raleigh Simms, the CEO of RES Communications. He's bidding on that big government contract. If he gets it, our phone service, cable service, all that stuff will go through his company.

This is a multi-billion-dollar deal he's working on. But it seems he's had a few problems keeping his hands to himself. Three of his staff are suing for sexual harassment."

"I just read an article about him the other day. He's almost a shoe-in for that deal. They're saying he has a lot of people on the Regulatory Committee in his pocket," Keith chimed in.

"That's him alright. Anyway, three of his staff—two women and one man—are suing him. A while back there was some fiasco about him cheating on his wife. That's not going to make our job any easier. This is going to be a tricky one." Charles nodded his head as if agreeing with himself.

"Why do you say that, Charles? We've defended sexual harassment before." Cienna gave him a questioning look.

"Yeah, but not this type of sexual harassment. You see, the two women were in line for a promotion. One got the promotion because she did what he asked. Later, she claimed it was involuntary and that she only gave in to keep her job. The other one flat out refused his advances and claims he physically assaulted her in his office. And the man, well, the man still works there, but he's been demoted twice since the filing of this suit." Charles leaned back in his chair, carefully watching the expression on both their faces.

"Damn, he's a freaky little bastard," Keith observed. "So, what do you want us to do?"

"I want you and Cienna to handle this one together. I think we'll need both the male and female advantage on this one." Cienna was astounded; Keith was intrigued.

"I think that we're both good enough that either of us could work the case alone. I mean, if we need to bounce ideas off one another, we're in the same office, so it wouldn't be a problem." Cienna desperately hoped Charles would reconsider. The last thing she wanted was to work closely with Keith.

"No, I want you to work together. I think it'll look good for the firm, too. It shows we're sympathetic to both sexes."

"No, it shows we're smart enough to know that it's going to take two people to pull Mr. Simms out of this mess. His wife should lock him away for all the times he's cheated on her," Keith commented.

Cienna frowned. The thought of infidelity grated on her nerves to no end.

"Now, let's be objective. These are just allegations. I've set a meeting for you two with Mr. Simms in his office tomorrow at three. I'm giving both of you a copy of the complaint and sworn statements from some of the people in the office, along with some other stuff you should look over. Review it, and review every other incident in which he has been accused of something. See me after you meet with him."

"Yes, sir," Keith answered before standing to leave. He noted that Cienna was still sitting. Damn, but she was fine. He and some of the other attorneys often talked about how good she looked, but everybody who'd asked her out had struck out.

Since he'd never accepted rejection well, Keith hadn't even tried. He'd simply watched her from a distance for the past year, wondering what it would be like to kiss her lips, to make love to her, to watch her reach her orgasm as he brought her undeniable pleasure.

He imagined taking her slowly, his lips canvassing every inch of her. He'd savor the taste of her before coming into her and pumping like mad to bring her to her first of many climaxes. His fingers itched to touch her breasts, to hold them in his hands and kiss the nipples till they strained against his fingertips.

When he'd walked into Charles' office, he'd been greeted by long, mocha-colored legs peeking from beneath a knee-length purple skirt. Her suit jacket buttoned just below two perfect breasts. Standing above her, Keith could see the swells of her smooth mounds. Her hair, always impeccable, softly framed her perfectly round face. Brown eyes, sensuously pouting lips and a killer smile summed up the complete package.

Keith could have devoured her in one bite. But she was his co-worker and as such, she needed to remain off limits. Office gossip was a huge source of entertainment at Benton and King, and he had no desire for his love life to be a lunchtime topic of discussion.

Besides, things could get sticky when it became time to part ways, and he definitely didn't need that drama at work.

"Cienna, are you okay with this arrangement?" Charles asked her.

"I'm just fine with it, sir. I'm sure Keith and I will work well together." Standing to leave the office, she carefully averted her eyes from Keith's direction. He held the door for her, and both men watched the sway of her hips as she walked out. Taking a deep, cleansing breath Keith turned to Charles.

"Don't thank me yet. She's a pistol," Charles warned, reading Keith's mind.

"So I've heard," Keith grinned. "But she's the best-looking pistol I've seen in a long time." At that, Charles joined Keith in laughing.

Mionne watched as Cienna walked back into her office. She waited exactly five minutes before she followed her in and shut the door. Mionne and Cienna had been friends since Mionne started with the firm three years ago. She secretly envied Cienna, but insisted that her perfect size-eight body and gorgeous skin had nothing to do with it. Full-figured Mionne felt the slight sting of jealousy. Still, she considered Cienna a friend. She hadn't had many friends in her lifetime.

"So, what did he want?" she asked, settling her healthy-sized body into the chair across from Cienna.

"I have to work with Keith on this big case," Cienna told her.

"Oh? That's not bad. I thought you were in trouble for something." Mionne breathed a sigh of relief.

"What do you mean, it's not bad? How am I supposed to work with him?" Cienna asked.

"Just do your job. Don't look at him. Don't smell him. Don't even acknowledge he's a man." Mionne reached for the candy jar on the end of Cienna's desk.

"That's stupid, Mionne. I have to acknowledge him, and you know once you acknowledge him there's no way you can ignore him." Cienna folded her hands on the desk, trying to figure out a way to deal with this newest obstacle.

"Girl, I know. When he walked past my desk today, my nipples got all hard, and my crotch got damp…"

"That's enough, Mionne. I don't think I have it that bad." Cienna eyed her friend suspiciously. "When's the last time you saw Lee anyway?" Lee was

Mionne's latest boyfriend. Cienna had never met Lee, but from the things that Mionne had told her about him, he sounded like a loser. She'd told Mionne as much when she first started seeing him. He didn't seem to have a lot of time to spend with Mionne, but the moment he called, she dropped everything and ran to wherever it was he wanted her to meet him. As far as Cienna knew, Mionne had never been to his place and knew very little about his life in general. Cienna thought he sounded like he was married, but didn't mention this to Mionne.

"Last night. Why?"

"Did he give you some? You seem awfully hot over there."

"Let me tell you about Lee. All he wants to do is lick the carpet. Girl, I'm sick of it."

"What's wrong with that?" Cienna asked, perplexed. She hadn't had her carpet licked in months, and it sounded pretty good right about now.

"No, you don't understand. Usually that's *all* he wants to do. No penetration, no nothing. Just lickin' for about fifteen or twenty minutes, then he's done. He's good though, girl. I be so wet I feel like a damn waterfall. And he sucks my clit like you wouldn't believe. He says he thinks about it all day and he gets his thing off from just seeing me pleased. But damn, I'd like to feel something inside besides his tongue.

You know what I mean?" Mionne asked. She chewed on the chocolate thoughtfully.

"No, I can't say I know what you mean, as I'm a bit dry down there these days," Cienna offered. The thought of her non-existent sex life further darkened her mood.

"If you'd stop working so hard and stop being so picky, you could get yourself a little piece."

"Yeah? It so happens I have other things to do besides get a little piece. Besides, when I get it, it damn sure better be a *big* piece." Cienna laughed, then said thoughtfully, "I'll bet Keith has a big piece."

"I'm sure he does. Have you seen his lips, girl? I'd settle for just lickin' with him," Mionne said as she got up to go.

"No, I think you should stick with Lee, Mionne," Cienna warned her friend. Mionne walked out of her office smiling.

CHAPTER THREE

Cienna flinched as the piercing buzzer sounded throughout her office; she silently prayed it wasn't Reka again. She had gone to lunch with her and had listened to the latest about Jeff and his brother's girlfriend, and she really didn't want to hear any more today.

Reka wore on her nerves. The more she tried to be nice to the girl, the more it seemed the girl irked her. Petty gossip seemed to be her lifeline and without it, Cienna was sure Reka would drop dead of boredom. The girl was twenty-two years old and lived in a little apartment just outside the downtown area. She'd had about twenty bad relationships in the three years Cienna had known her. And no matter how many times Cienna had tried to lecture her about saving herself—saving her love for someone special—Reka never seemed to listen. Every guy she met was "the one," and every relationship was headed towards marriage, but each relationship failed within eight weeks. Cienna didn't know what else to say to the girl.

"Yes?" she answered hesitantly.

"Cienna? It's Keith. I wanted to see if you were available to meet tomorrow morning so we can get our thoughts together before the meeting with Simms." His voice filled the office and filtered through her body like fine wine, slow and silky. Something she didn't want to feel. But he had a good idea, and she couldn't very well run from the man. Her job was too important to her for her to jeopardize it over a man again. She could handle this situation; she was a strong black woman. For whatever good it did her, right now she was a horny black woman fighting the attraction to a sexy black man.

"Yeah, that sounds good. How about ten?" she asked.

"Ten's good," he answered. Then there was silence.

"Was there something else?" Cienna prompted.

"Oh, no. Um, ten's fine. I'll see you then," he said, reluctantly hanging up. You would have thought they were in two different buildings. He was only on the other side of the same building; it would take him exactly two minutes to walk from his office to hers. So if he liked hearing her voice, he could just walk on over there and continue the conversation in person. Or, he could stay right where he was and keep his pride intact. He decided to go with the latter.

It was a quarter-after-five, and Keith knew the office would be substantially quieter, as almost everybody would have gone home. He left his office to go to the kitchen to get a drink and some chips. That would have to tide him over until he could get home and get something more substantial, which wouldn't be for at least another two hours. There was a brief on his desk that demanded his attention.

Cienna was in the kitchen hastily rinsing out her coffee cup. She was having dinner at her parents' house tonight, and she didn't dare be late, as that would only prolong the evening. As she turned to leave, she ran smack into Keith, the last person she wanted to see tonight.

"Ooops! Excuse me."

"I'm sorry, I wasn't even looking."

They spoke in unison. He stepped to the side out of her way. She stepped in the same direction. He moved to the other side; she moved to the same side. They giggled as they tried again to move out of each other's way, their sides brushing slightly against each other. When they had successfully cleared the path, they both stood still, refusing to acknowledge the bolts of electricity going through them after their brief contact.

"I'm off for the night. So, I'll see you in the morning." Cienna attempted to make her exit.

"Wait!" The sound of his voice caused her to halt before reaching the doorway.

"What? Is there something wrong?" she asked, slightly alarmed.

"No, I, ah, I just, um, I was wondering how you really feel about us working together." That wasn't what he was wondering at all. He was really wondering how long it would take him to get her out of that suit and onto that table with her legs spread wide and his face between them.

"It's fine. I mean, I've worked with other associates in the office on cases before. It's no big deal," she lied. It was actually a great big deal, considering the other associates weren't half as attractive as this man was. Long, elegant fingers led the way to strong, wide palms. She ached to feel those hands on her.

"Good, 'cause I'm hoping we can do a bang-up job on this one. It'd be one more step to the big time."

"What? You mean a partnership? Is that what you want out of this?" she asked him, curious now about the man beneath the suit.

"Nah. A partnership would definitely help, but I really want to be a judge."

"Oh, I see." She did see. He had goals—goals that probably, much like her own, came before anything else.

"You see what?" Watching her quizzically, he wondered what was going on in that pretty little head of hers.

"I just hadn't realized you aimed so high." Shrugging her shoulders, she decided to downplay the brownie points he'd just scored with her.

"Why not? Don't you?"

"Of course. But I've set my sights on partner for now. I'll think about the rest when I make it that far." Cienna wasn't sure why she was sharing this with him. Until now, only her parents had known her true aspirations, but she'd confided in him as easily as if she'd known him all her life.

"Really? I've heard good things about your work, so I'm sure you'll get there soon." Keith's primary goal had always been to be a judge. Everything else took a backseat. His mother was always pushing him to fall in love, get married and make some babies. But none of that appealed to him. Not yet anyway. "What about your personal life?"

"I'm not much on personal life. It's pretty time consuming." She thought she saw a flicker of disappointment in his eyes, but it quickly vanished. She remembered a time when she had been consumed by her personal life and the price she had paid for that mistake.

"To each his own," he said finally. "But I think we'll work well together. I'm going to try to look through the file tonight so I'll be ready for our meeting in the morning."

"Yeah, I'm gonna look at it tonight, too. So, I guess I'll see you in the morning." He watched her turn to walk away, his breath hitching with the gentle sway of her hips.

"Okay, goodnight," she called as she rounded the corner to the hallway.

"Goodnight," he said to her back. He sat down and tried to figure out what had just happened. *Was she attracted to him?* It almost appeared so, but he couldn't be sure. The swelling in his pants confirmed what he already knew: He wanted her, badly.

Still, it didn't seem that either one of them had time for a relationship. But that didn't rule out some nice steamy sex, he thought. He contemplated how he would go about making that happen.

Cienna sat in her car wondering about Keith Page. She'd thought she had him figured out. Reka, as well as the rest of the office, had kept her informed on how many women called the office for him, so she had just assumed that he was into dating and all that other stuff. But now it seemed to her that Mr. Page was just about work. She wondered why that thought was so unsettling. After all, she didn't have any real interest in him anyway. She wanted to be a partner, despite his blasé attitude about it. That was her goal, and she would fulfill it. Then she would find herself a man and settle down. *Maybe.*

She knew he'd been watching her walk away; she could feel it as her butt cheeks warmed. It pleased her to know that he was looking at her that way. She could do worse than attract a man like Keith.

CHAPTER FOUR

"Girl, Lee was on the money last night. He hit all the right places and then some," Mionne lounged in the chair in Cienna's office as she gave her the sultry details of her rendezvous the previous night.

"Oh, really? You mean he didn't just eat and run this time?" Cienna flipped through Mr. Simms' file one more time.

"Ha-ha, very funny," Mionne snickered. "Of course he did. But he did a damn good job of it. I'm not complaining. No, not at all." She remembered how Lee had been waiting for her when she'd walked in the door. She'd gone into her bedroom and was taking her clothes off when he came in and finished taking her stockings off for her. It had started right there in the closet. When he'd bent down to ease her panties off, he'd stayed down, burying his face between her legs as his tongue explored the moist lips of her vagina, causing her to go limp in his arms.

"Ah, excuse me, miss, but if you're having a moment, can you please have it at your own desk?" Cienna said to her friend who had gotten all glossy-eyed and quiet. "I have an appointment at ten."

"Oh, yeah. I noticed that on your calendar." Mionne eyed her suspiciously. "I also noticed that you're wearing an awfully tight skirt, and that blouse leaves nothing to the imagination." Mionne raised one heavily-painted eyebrow in Cienna's direction.

Cienna defended her outfit. "What are you talking about? My skirt is not too tight, and my blouse, while it may be a bit sheer, is very professional and goes well with this particular suit." It had taken her twenty minutes to pick it out this morning. The navy blue suit was both professional and sexy, and the cream-colored shell barely showed the lacy beige camisole she wore underneath. It hugged her in all the right places, she had to admit, but if Mr. Page were so sure of his goals in life, it wouldn't bother him in the least bit.

"Yeah, right. I see what you're doing. I'll just warn you to watch out."

"Watch out for what?" she asked, curious now at Mionne's warning.

"I hear he's just coming out of a long-term relationship that didn't end too well," Mionne whispered.

"Where'd you hear that?"

"Reka told me yesterday that just last week, the woman called him several times, and when he finally took the call, she stood in Jerry's office and listened through the wall. She heard him telling her it was over, that he could get sex from anywhere, that he didn't need hers, and all that. Just watch yourself cause he's a smooth one." Keith's broad body filled the doorway just as Mionne stood to leave.

"Good morning, Mionne." He smiled down at her.

"Good morning, Keith." Mionne smiled right back at him. "Oooh, you smell good this morning. You got a hot lunch date or something?" Mionne purposely glanced towards Cienna and winked at her as she left the office.

"She's something, isn't she?" Keith said. He came in and shut Cienna's door.

"Something is not the word for Mionne." Cienna took a whiff of his cologne. He did smell good. She decided she'd better get right down to business. "So, did you get a chance to look through the file?"

"Yeah. But I'm more concerned about the previous allegations than this one. I mean, I know they can't use them at trial, but they definitely taint his credibility."

Cienna studied Keith as he took a seat across from her. He had left his suit jacket in his office. His white shirt was crisply starched and complemented with a yellow silk tie and sage green pants which tapered around his waist perfectly. His wing-tipped shoes gleamed from beneath an inch of cuffed material. He wore a gold watch (TAG Heuer, Cienna suspected), and what looked like his school ring on his left hand.

"I know what you mean. I had the same concerns myself. Mr. Simms definitely has a problem keeping his hands to himself. And now, it seems he's graduated from women to more creative means of satisfaction." Cienna was referring to the advances he had made towards his IT assistant, Paul Barber, who happened to be a gay white man.

"I don't even want to think about that right now. It's too early in the morning. And besides, I've already talked to Tacoma, so I've exceeded my daily dosage of weirdness for one day." They both laughed.

"Tacoma is a sweet guy," Cienna added before getting up to cross the office. The remainder of her file was on the chair by the door.

"Yeah, you women like gay men, don't you? I think it's only because you don't have to worry about them coming on to you." He watched Cienna smile. She was so pretty; he could sit and stare at her all day, especially today. When she'd gotten up to retrieve the rest of her file, he'd noticed how her skirt had snuggled her butt closely and hugged her hips. He'd even glimpsed a small wisp of lace that covered her breasts. Damn! It was going to be a task keeping his mind on Raleigh Simms and his indiscretions when he was contemplating a few indiscretions of his own.

"That's always a plus, but that's not the only reason. They're just nice to talk to; they give you the pretense of talking to a man, but they have the mind of a woman. It's kind of neat, actually," she told him. She sat back down behind her desk and opened her file.

"Yeah, I bet it is. So, you'd rather talk to a gay man than a straight man?" he asked out of curiosity.

"It depends on what we're talking about," she answered thoughtfully. "If I wanted an opinion on what to wear to the Lawyers' Ball, I would ask a gay man. On the other hand, if I wanted to know how good I looked in that particular outfit, I would ask a straight man."

"Who'd no doubt tell you how gorgeous you looked just to get you in bed," Keith added.

"Exactly." She laughed again. "But who knows, depending on the straight man I asked, that might have been the response I was looking for." *Why had she said that?* The room had instantly shifted from comfortable workplace to a small room with two very attractive, very horny people occupying it.

"Oh? So if you asked a man to tell you how good you looked, that would be like an invitation for him?" Keith watched her, his gaze smoldering.

"It could be. Like I said, it all depends on the man." Cienna found herself staring at him with equal intensity. Before he could say another word, Reka's voice echoed over the intercom, killing the mood.

"Keith?"

"Yes, Reka?" Keith said with an irritated look on his face.

"Tyra, line two." Reka's voice sounded as if she were smiling, but judging from the look on Keith's face, Cienna guessed he was anything but happy.

"I'm in a meeting, Reka." He put his head down and thumbed through the file on his lap.

"She doesn't want voicemail. Shall I leave her on hold again?"

"Do whatever you like, Reka." Pulling out a newspaper clipping, he passed it on to Cienna.

"Alright, remember you said that. Cee, you're my witness." Reka disconnected the line.

"You know she's gonna hang up on her, don't you?" Cienna barely masked her amusement.

"Good, then maybe she'll stop calling." He kept his face buried in the file. He didn't want her to think he was involved with anyone. Not that she was thinking of him in that way, but just in case she was.

"Maybe you shouldn't have given her your work number," Cienna mentioned, skimming the newspaper clipping he had given her.

"Maybe I shouldn't have gone out with her in the first place."

"Maybe you should try choosing your dates a little more carefully," Cienna said in a stiff tone. When he didn't respond, she looked up from the paper she had been reading to find him staring at her.

"Maybe I should," was his reply.

"Good afternoon. I'm Cienna Turner, and this is Keith Page. We have a three o'clock appointment with Mr. Simms."

"Oh, yes. He's waiting for you. You can go right in," the receptionist said. She was chewing gum, sounding like a big cow, but her chewing stopped when she saw Keith. "Just go through that door. It's the first office on your right." She now gave Keith a full seduction smile that showed off her gleaming gold tooth.

"I think you have an admirer," Cienna said. She nodded toward the receptionist behind them.

"What gives you that idea?" Keith asked with a cocky grin.

"You just love it, don't you?"

"Love what?" He smiled, showing off one deep dimple in his right cheek.

"Women drooling all over you. It just pumps your little ego right up."

"Nah, I don't really pay that much attention to it. Besides, she's not my type," he said seriously.

"And just what is your type, counselor?" She was suddenly very curious about what type of woman attracted Keith Page.

"You're the closest thing to my type that I've seen in a long time." He was looking at her that way again. The same way he had looked at her earlier in the office—as if he could see right through her.

"Yeah, right." She stepped back to give herself space to breathe or run if necessary. She hadn't expected that response, and she wasn't quite sure how to react to it.

They arrived at the door and knocked briefly before going in.

As they entered, a woman hurried past Cienna and Keith. She looked, from Cienna's brief assessment of her, to be significantly younger than Simms, and she was attempting to adjust the short skirt she wore.

Raleigh Simms a short, stout man who looked to be on the closer side of sixty, stood behind his desk adjusting his tie, breathing a little erratically.

Keith looked at Cienna. Cienna looked at Keith. Their eyes spoke the comments that raced through both their minds.

"Well, hello. You must be the attorneys from Benton's firm. Come on in," he said jovially.

Keith figured he'd be in a damn good mood, too, if he'd just screwed a woman on the desk in his office. Well, not just any woman. He found himself staring at Cienna, thinking of having her on top of a desk.

Cienna found herself staring at the man behind the desk. He looked vaguely familiar, but she couldn't

quite place his face. She'd probably seen him on television or his picture in the paper. RES was negotiating
a major deal in the state right now, so he was probably
very visible to the public.

"I'm Cienna Turner, and this is Keith Page,"
Cienna said as Keith closed the office door behind
them.

Simms leaned over his desk to shake their hands
briefly. As he took his seat, Cienna wiped her hands
on her clothing. Keith did the same and tried not to
laugh. They sat in the two chairs directly across from
the desk.

"So, shall we get started?" Simms asked.

Keith looked at Cienna. Cienna looked at Keith.
They both turned their noses up at the distinct smell
of sex that lingered in the room.

"Is something wrong?" Simms asked.

"Ah, no, nothing at all. Let's start with the
obvious," Keith said. Cienna thought she would fall
out of her chair. Surely he was not about to say what
she thought. Please, Lord, don't let it be so.

"And what is the obvious, Mr....What was your
name again?"

"Page, Keith Page. And by the obvious, sir, I
simply mean the allegations. What do you think
brought the allegations about?" Keith spoke smoothly.
He'd seen Cienna's panic-stricken face out of the
corner of his eye and suppressed a grin.

"Oh, yes, the allegations. I'll start by saying they are completely false and out of line. I would never do such a thing. I'm a business man and a public figure." Simms waved his hand through the air as if to dismiss all other questions.

Cienna and Keith looked at each other once again and did everything in their power not to laugh in the man's face. If nothing else, this was going to be an interesting case.

CHAPTER FIVE

"Good morning, how may I help you?" Reka asked the thin woman who stood in front of her.

"I'd like to see Mionne Steward, please." The woman spoke in a quiet, nervous tone.

Reka called Mionne to the front desk. A few minutes later, Mionne came around the corner and greeted the woman tersely. The woman barely nodded towards Mionne before handing her a slip of paper.

When Mionne accepted the paper, the woman immediately went to the elevator and pushed the button. When it stopped, she got in without saying another word. Mionne unfolded the paper and read it. Rolling her eyes skyward, she turned and walked away.

Reka sat behind her computer and pretended to be into her game of solitaire as she took in everything that occurred. The whole scene was strange, and she didn't know what to make of it. She'd discuss it with Tacoma at lunch today. Maybe he'd have some information that would shed some light on this incident.

And if he didn't, once she brought it to his attention he'd do his best to find out what was going on.

Mionne went to the third floor of the building, just as the note had instructed. It was one-thirty, so she was on time. But there was no one here. She looked around. This floor had housed a personnel agency a few months back. Now, it was just empty office space.

A sound came from one of the offices towards the back. Mionne jumped and stared intently in that direction. When a man who looked to be in his early thirties stepped into the doorway, her racing heart calmed a bit.

"You're right on time—I like that." The man, who was wearing a business suit, smiled at her. He motioned for her to join him in the office, and she obliged.

When she was in the office, he closed the door behind them, clicking the lock in place. He didn't hesitate but moved swiftly, taking her by the waist roughly.

Mionne closed her eyes and let his hands roam all over her body. He grabbed at her breasts, filling his hands with their heaviness. At the same time, he ground his pelvis into her hips, rubbing his arousal urgently against her midsection.

He groaned. She whimpered. His hands found hers and guided them to his swollen sex. She gripped him tightly in her hands, at first through the material of his pants. Then, she slid the zipper down to release him. When the long length of his shaft was in her hand, skin-to-skin, she stroked him ardently.

He moaned, "Take it, baby."

Once again Mionne obliged, going down on her knees. She took him into her mouth slowly, completely. He sucked in his breath and buried his hands in her hair. She began to move, pleasuring him beyond belief. When she felt the telltale throbbing of his engorged sex, she pulled her mouth away, stroking him persistently with her hands until hot waves of cream-colored liquid oozed onto her hands.

"Was that what you wanted?" Her voice was cool as she searched for something to wipe her hands on.

Fixing his pants, the man looked down at her. "It sure was. I got exactly what I requested."

Mionne couldn't find anything that resembled a tissue. She wished she hadn't left her purse upstairs in her desk. Leaning over, she wiped her hands on the carpet, then stood to leave.

Back on the ninth floor, she headed straight for the bathroom. Reka and Tacoma were standing at the front desk when she walked by.

"Umph, office quickie." Reka looked at Tacoma.

"You know it," Tacoma grinned. He held his hand up in the air, and Reka nodded in agreement, giving him a high five.

"Cienna?" Keith spoke over the intercom connection to Cienna's office. There was no answer. He disconnected, wondering if she were even in today. He hadn't chanced going to that side of the office for fear of running into her before he had time to figure out what he was going to say, how he was going to act. All of the sexual overtures of the previous day had made him realize that he wanted Cienna even more than he had first thought. His night had been restless. He had tried to work, then tried to sleep, but alas, visions of her beneath him or on top of him overwhelmed his mind. When he'd finally drifted off, it was with undeniable lust for her bitter on his tongue.

"Keith?" Reka called into his office.

"Yeah?" he answered bleakly.

"Tyra McKenzie on line three." Reka anxiously awaited his response.

"Voicemail," he said quickly. "Oh, and can you page Cienna and have her call me?" He knew that just by that general request, he was likely starting the buzz about him and Cienna. They *were* working together on a case, though, so he had the perfect alibi.

"I sure will," Reka said all too happily. In the next instant, Keith heard Reka's voice throughout the office.

"Cienna Turner, call the front desk, please."

He waited a few moments for the phone to ring. Sitting in his office, he had rehearsed what he was going to say and needed to say it before he lost his nerve. Damn, this woman was something. He hadn't been this nervous about a female since middle school, and here she had him planning what to say and hoping that she would respond affirmatively.

"Keith?" Cienna's voice sounded in his ears.

His hands didn't shake as he picked up the receiver, but his throat was suddenly very dry. "Hey, Cienna. I was just wondering if you'd like to grab some lunch and talk about our next step with Simms." He spoke quickly, then held his breath in anticipation of her response. He badly wanted her to say yes. He knew he was being silly; she was only a woman—but a woman who had successfully invaded his dreams for the past couple of nights.

"That's fine. Where do you want to go?" she asked casually.

"Ah, anywhere's fine with me. How about Mo's?" He was beginning to sweat. She sounded so business-like, so impersonal. However, he had said he wanted to discuss the case. It wasn't as if he had asked her out on a date.

"Okay, I'll meet you at the front desk in about fifteen minutes," she said before she hung up.

Keith let out a deep breath and used his fifteen minutes to plan what they would talk about at lunch. The case, of course, but there was so much more he wanted to know about her, and he knew she wouldn't volunteer any information. He had to come up with a clever way of getting it out of her.

For her part, Cienna sat in the conference room where she had been working, wondering what she was going to say to him for a whole hour. Going out to lunch was almost like a date, except that it was her case—the case they would most likely be discussing the case, the case being Simms and his horny fat ass. The picture she had conjured up from the scene in his office stuck in her mind like a piece of popcorn lodged between her teeth: Simms slumped over the woman, heaving as if he were about to have a heart attack. She shook her head vigorously in an attempt to push it aside. She had thought about it all night, sort of. But not just Simms and his insatiable appetite for sex. She had also conjured up images of herself and Keith sharing similar activities. In self-defense she had chosen to work in the conference room today just in case he stopped by her office wanting to talk, which she was sure he had. Otherwise, Reka would not have paged her.

But she would survive lunch. They'd talk about work, and that would be it. As long as they kept it simple, she'd survive.

She would not make the same mistake twice. She had vowed years ago that she wouldn't be a fool again, and even though Keith was wreaking havoc on her composure, she *would* remain professional. And so would their relationship.

CHAPTER SIX

Keith was already at the front desk. Today, he was dressed in a dark brown suit and a perfectly pressed shirt the color of freshly churned butter. His tie displayed shades of brown, beige and gold and perfectly accented the ensemble. He had been leaning over the desk talking to Reka when Cienna rounded the corner. She hesitated a moment, almost turning to walk in the opposite direction, but Reka saw her.

"Hey Cienna, where you been hidin' all mornin'?" Reka asked cheerfully.

"I was working in Conference Room B. I needed to spread some things out." Cienna tried not to look at Keith. "Are you ready?" She finally allowed her gaze to meet his. He stared at her with such intensity that she almost jumped on him right there in the lobby.

"Yup." He pushed the down arrow to signal the elevator.

"We'll be back in about an hour," Cienna said to Reka.

"Take your time. It's a pretty day outside. Go for a walk or something," Reka added.

"Why thank you, boss. Remember that when it's time to sign my paycheck," Cienna said as the elevator doors closed, blocking her view of Reka's smug face.

"She's a pill," Keith observed when they were alone in the elevator.

"Yeah, she's that and then some." There wasn't enough room in the elevator. Keith was taking up all the space, and Cienna felt as if he had pushed her into a corner.

Keith watched her squirm once they were alone. His ego inflated another few inches at the thought that he made her nervous. He would have purposely provoked more squirming had he not been as jittery as a schoolboy himself.

She wore a gray pantsuit today with a vibrant blue blouse beneath the jacket. The shirt began to button just at the swell of her breasts, which were rising and falling with each breath she took. He knew he shouldn't look, but he couldn't help himself. He lifted his arm to stare at his watch and quickly glanced at the opening of her blouse where the creamy brown skin separated into two perfect mounds. He imagined his tongue in that exact spot and gulped for air.

"After you, madam," he said hoarsely as the doors opened into the lobby of the building. Cienna stepped out and began to walk towards the door. She knew he was watching her walk and decided to give him something to stare at. The extra-added sway of her hips must have been ample entertainment, because when she turned around to see him, he was cursing as the elevator doors were closing with him in between them. *Gotcha!* She smiled and turned away so he wouldn't see her triumph.

In the restaurant, they sat at a table in the back by the window. It was crowded, as it was lunchtime and Mo's was a popular spot. Cienna didn't need to go over the menu; she almost knew it by heart. Besides, she always ordered the same thing—one broiled crab cake and a baked sweet potato.

"I'll have the seafood platter with a side salad," Keith said after she had given the waiter her order. He liked a decisive woman, and Cienna was definitely that. She didn't look at him with that whimpering child look and ask him what he thought she should have. She ordered her food and waited for him to do the same.

"Okay, so what do you think so far?" he asked after the waiter had left.

"From most of the statements from the staff, I think it's safe to say that there is definitely a hostile work environment. And that alone is grounds enough for the lawsuit," she said matter-of-factly.

"Yeah, I got the same impression. But at the time these particular incidents occurred, there were no reports made to any supervisors. That's at least something," Keith added.

"Who do you tell if the CEO is the one initiating the advances?"

"I guess you're right about that, but wouldn't you tell *somebody?* I mean, wouldn't *you* tell?"

"You mean, if you started making unwanted sexual advances towards me right now, would I run back to the office and tell Charles?" She watched him closely over the rim of her water glass.

"Assuming the advances were unwanted, yes, would you tell Charles?" He was curious now. He wanted to know the boundaries that lay between them.

"You're damn right I would." She carefully put her glass on the table. "But if the advances were welcome, or should I say foreseeable, then we'd have an even bigger problem." She could tell exactly what he was thinking. There was no way that the sexual attraction between the two of them was just one-sided. He felt precisely what she did. She was sure of it. And that had nothing to do with her ego.

"Really?" He wondered just what she'd do if he kissed her. No, that would be moving too fast; he'd try something a little subtler. "So, what, exactly, do you consider an advance? I mean, if I were to say...touch your hand like this...," he reached across the table and placed his hand on top of hers, "...would that be an advance?"

Cienna tried not to jerk away, but the heat between them seemed to engulf the room. "That would be a casual advance, yes," she answered.

"And if I did this..." He lifted her hand to his mouth. His thick damp lips brushed over her knuckles slowly, sensuously, before he placed her hand back on the table. "That would be what? A more forward advance?" His eyes never left hers, and he watched the signs of passion seep into the pools of brown.

"That would be borderline sexual." Now, had he taken each finger one by one into his mouth, that would have definitely been sexual. But she wasn't going to tell him that. Let him figure it out for himself. "Now if I, say, put my hand here...," she scooted a little in her chair until she was close enough to him to place her hand on his knee, "...what would you consider that?"

Keith felt a familiar tightening in his groin and almost shuddered. "I would call that a definite sexual overture," he said through clenched teeth. He wasn't sure what they were doing now, but it was unquestionably getting hot in there.

"And any motion of my hand would increase the seriousness of that overture. Am I right?" Cienna asked. He wasn't the only one who could play the game. They were in a crowded restaurant and, therefore, completely safe from taking things too far.

Keith cleared his throat. "Cienna, I think we should stop with this little hypothesis for the moment."

"Okay. So suppose it went down like that and Barber said the exact same thing you said, which in essence, he did. I mean, he didn't jump up and hit him, and he didn't curse him or tell him he was completely out of line. So doesn't that say that the action wasn't entirely unwanted?"

"Ah, I guess, I mean, I guess we could say that." Keith was having a hard time thinking as Cienna hadn't moved her hand yet, and he didn't know how to ask her to. He had never had to tell a woman not to touch him before, especially not when he really wanted her to continue touching him. "But silence doesn't always equal consent."

"Yeah, that's the tricky part," she said as their food arrived. Cienna paused a moment to say grace. Keith watched her bow her head and felt a new feeling come over him. The heat had all but passed when she removed her hand. Now there was a sort of stirring inside him.

Of all the dates he'd been on, this was the first time the woman had paused to bless her food. He was deeply impressed and falling for Cienna Turner more and more by the minute.

"You know, there's a case that made it to the Supreme Court that involved unprotested intercourse on more than forty occasions. The argument was that conduct which might not have been unwelcome at the time can still be claimed unwanted at any future time." He paused to take a bite of salad. "So if what's his name, John Barber, was feeling a little adventurous on Tuesday and decided to let the passes go, then on Friday figured he wasn't quite into this, he's well within his rights to claim harassment, and the courts would likely side with him."

"Okay. So what about *quid pro quo*? Barber wanted a promotion and a raise. Maybe Simms said sure, if he gave him something in return. You think that's the situation here?" Cienna was putting butter on her baked potato when some got on her finger and she licked it off. It wasn't like she was on a date. She was completely at ease with Keith in that regard. She didn't feel she had to do anything to impress him or that she had to hide unsightly habits from him until later in the relationship. She could just be herself for now, like it or not.

But Keith was experiencing quite a reaction to her natural instinct. He had watched, mesmerized, as her lips enclosed her finger and it slid back out again with an undeniable sheen of moisture. "That's something we need to investigate further. The sooner we can rule that out, the better off we'll be," he said, concentrating unnecessarily on his plate.

"That'll take some time," she said thoughtfully. Time they'd undoubtedly have to spend together. She wondered at her true feelings about that situation.

She couldn't help being reminded of certain business lunches in the past; business lunches that had eventually led to evening discussions; evening discussions that had led to overnights; overnights that had ultimately led to the beginning of a serious relationship—a serious relationship that had collapsed in one afternoon.

Cienna and Keith lingered at the table, stuffed from their meal and thoughtful of the personal step they had taken. They had tested and confirmed what each had already suspected: they were sexually attracted to each other. How they were going to deal with that was another story entirely.

Although Cienna wanted to put it aside and concentrate on the case, she couldn't ignore the thrill she'd felt watching him writhe at her touch. A part of her wanted to go further with him—a big part of her.

Another part wanted to protect her feelings by keeping herself distant and remote from any personal involvement. Hadn't she and Bobby started out the same way? She concluded that there was a distinct possibility that this would be a repeat of that situation.

Then, there was the professional angle. She shouldn't risk an office affair; she had too much to lose.

Keith watched her attentively; he could almost see what was going on in that pretty little head of hers. She was weighing the odds. Should they sleep together, or should they concentrate on being colleagues and nothing more? He was having a similar battle himself. For him, the answer was no less complicated. While he was fairly certain he could get her into his bed and even more certain that they would both enjoy it, he worried about the consequences of those actions.

Cienna didn't look like the romp-and-roll type, but he didn't think she was considering a long-term relationship either. It would definitely get sticky at work. Somebody would find out, and then what would happen? Even so, with all that in the mix, the hardest chunk for him to swallow was that he wasn't sure he wanted just a roll in the sack with her.

"So counselor, it looks like we have our work cut out for us," she said finally.

"Yeah, it appears so." He noticed that her eyes were a little further apart than a normal person's but that they were slanted naturally, giving her an exotic look. The words suddenly came out before he could stop them. "I'd like to take you out on a real date."

Cienna stared at him for a moment before responding. "I don't think that's a good idea," she said, wanting more than anything to say yes.

"I knew you'd say that."

"So why'd you bring it up?" She hoped she was giving him the impression that she wasn't interested.

"Because I think it's time we put all our cards on the table, so to speak. I'm interested in you beyond the workplace, and I'm pretty sure you're equally interested in me. Correct me if I'm wrong," he said, as he prayed he wasn't wrong.

Cienna wished she could tell him he was wrong, but that would be a lie. "No, you're right about the attraction. But it's impossible, and we both know it. We have an agenda, and an involvement between us isn't included on it."

"I don't know about you, but my agenda's written in pencil, so changes aren't a problem." And at that moment, he realized he would amend it any way he could to include her.

"I just don't think it's a good idea. I mean, what happens after we sleep together?" she asked.

"I didn't ask to sleep with you. I asked you for a date." He cleared that up for her, deciding he would tackle sleeping with her at a later time.

"One will inevitably lead lead to the other," she countered. She noticed his hands as he gripped the glass of soda and took a sip. They were large but without calluses, and his nails were clean. That was a plus in her book.

"I don't argue that fact. But I'd like to start off slowly and work my way up to sleeping with you." He smiled a smooth, genuine smile that only enhanced his good looks and displayed a small dimple in his left cheek.

"You talk like you know it's going to happen," she said, amused. Bobby had always been sure about himself, too.

"I do. And you know it, too. So what do you say to a movie and dinner?" he asked, watching her intently as she struggled to turn him down.

"I don't know. I'll have to think about this more," she said finally.

"The more you think about it, the harder it will be to make the decision." The waiter approached as he said that. "I'll take the check, thanks." He withdrew his wallet from his back pocket.

"We could have used the firm's expense account for this," she said, motioning towards the gold card he had casually placed on the table.

"I know, but I figured if I paid for it myself, we could consider this our first date, so when I pick you up on Friday, you won't be nervous because that would actually be our second date." He smiled as she opened her mouth to say something and quickly shut it again.

CHAPTER SEVEN

It was already Friday, and Cienna had yet to figure out a way to get out of her date with Keith. She had thought about it the last few days and couldn't come up with an excuse that wouldn't sound like, well...like an excuse.

He had kept his distance since their lunch, and she was thankful for that, but time was ticking down quickly. At around ten this morning, she had finally admitted that she was scared. She was afraid of what this could lead to and, at the same time, afraid not to try and find out what it could lead to. She didn't like being afraid, and she detested backing down from a challenge. And Keith was definitely a challenge.

"Girl, let me tell you what happened last night," Mionne started as she walked into Cienna's office and took a seat. "That damn Lee comes over about eight o'clock and wants to get down. I said, 'Look, we gotta talk about this relationship and where it's leading." Mionne finally noticed that Cienna was staring blankly at the fish tank that sat on an oak stand across from her desk and halted her monologue. "What's wrong with you?" she asked.

"What? Oh, hey girl. What's goin' on?" Cienna began shifting papers around on her desk.

"I just asked you the same thing. You look a little spaced out. Is something wrong?" Mionne scooted to the end of the chair to get a closer look at Cienna. Her ample breasts were propped up on the edge of the desk now as she surveyed her friend closer.

"No. I'm cool. How about you?" Cienna stopped moving and stared at her friend. She considered Mionne a friend, unlike Reka, who she liked but only considered a co-worker. Cienna was careful not to say too much to Reka, as she knew that as fast as it came from her mouth, Reka would have it spread throughout the office. But Mionne was different. She was more mature, and Cienna knew she could trust her. But she didn't want to talk about what was going on in her mind just yet. She wanted a while longer to try to figure things out for herself before bringing someone else into the equation.

"You don't look cool. You look flustered and edgy," Mionne stated. "Now I wonder who could have you feeling flustered?" Mionne sat back in her chair and waited for Cienna to tell her the truth.

"Nobody has me flustered. I have a lot going on right now, and I'm just a bit overwhelmed," Cienna answered. "This case with Keith is really important, and I don't want to mess it up. But it's a real sticky one," she finished, hoping that would be enough information to satisfy Mionne. She should have known better.

"You never wig out over a case. You're good, and you know it, even if it's a tough case." Mionne continued to stare at Cienna, who was now sitting back in her chair toying with a pen she had been pretending to write with. "So why don't you tell me the real story?"

"I might as well," Cienna sighed. "I'll end up telling you at some point anyway." Giving up, she walked across the room and closed the door to her office. Once back behind her desk she kicked off the three-inch heels that she had been in since seven o'clock this morning and plopped back down in her chair. Her hair was in loose curls today, and one heavy brown lock fell over her eye just as she began to speak.

"Well...," she said, and then momentarily paused to tuck the wayward strand behind her ear. "You know I've been working with Keith?"

"Yeah."

"And, you know that Keith is...he's Keith," Cienna said for lack of a better way to describe him.

"Yeah, I know that, too." Mionne rolled her eyes. "Damn, that's one good-looking man." She gripped her knees and gently massaged them.

"Can I tell this story, please?" Cienna asked a now drooling Mionne.

"I'm sorry. Go on." Mionne clasped her hands and held them still on her lap. Cienna watched Mionne's attempt at control. She wanted to laugh, but the situation was too serious.

"Thank you. Anyway, we've had to spend a considerable amount of time together working, and the case is a sexual harassment case which makes things a little...how do I put it...?" Cienna paused in search of the right words.

"It makes things a little tense, especially since you two are tiptoeing around your attraction for each other," Mionne finished. "Is that what you're trying to say?"

"Damn, you're good," Cienna exclaimed.

"I know it. Now keep going." Mionne waved her hand for Cienna to continue.

"So the other day we went out to lunch, and things sort of got a little sticky."

"What do you mean, *sticky*?" Mionne raised a perfectly arched eyebrow.

"I mean, we were talking about the case and how the incident could have gone down, when we started to role play a little." Cienna's voice hitched on the last word.

"Role play? Hmmm. Go on."

"So I was touching him and he was touching me, and we were both getting slightly involved in the touching and then he asked me out."

"But you were already out. I don't understand."

"No, we went out to lunch to discuss *the case,* so technically that wasn't out. It didn't really count. But then he goes and changes channels and wants to take me out, like on a real date."

"So, what did you say?" Mionne asked, once again, living vicariously through her friend.

"I told him it wasn't a good idea. What if people around here found out I went on a date with him? Then all the other geeks in here I've turned down will get their boxers all in a bunch and ask me out again. I don't need that kind of attention, nor do I want it."

"I see. So you'll turn down a date that you do want just because you're afraid of something you don't want happening when you're not even sure that will happen in the first place," Mionne deduced.

"What did you just say?"

"I said you're an idiot if you don't go on the date. The hell with the rest of the people around here! You turned them down 'cause you weren't interested. Now, you're interested in somebody—definitely inter-ested—and so is he, so why shouldn't you give it a try? It's just a date," Mionne said simply.

"I don't think it'll be just a date. You didn't feel the heat we were giving off in that restaurant. I mean, the air fairly sizzled with it. I'm not so sure we'll be able to keep a lid on it when we're not on the clock." Cienna folded her hands and rested her chin on them, contemplating her next step.

"Judging from the way you look and the way Keith's looked the last two days, I'm not sure you'll be able to keep a lid on it whether you're on the clock or not."

The intercom buzzer went off, and Keith's voice filled the room. "Cienna?"

Cienna almost jumped out of her chair as Mionne smiled knowingly. "Yes?" Cienna said. She picked up the receiver, as Mionne didn't need to hear their conversation. She knew too much already.

"I'm gonna head out for the day, but I wanted to remind you about tonight. I'll pick you up at seven. Is that okay?"

All at once, she decided to forget all the reasons for not going out with Keith. "Ah, yeah. That's fine. You know how to get to my apartment?"

"Yup, I've got the address right here, courtesy of our employee directory. So, I'll see you then."

"Okay, see you then." She placed the receiver back in its cradle.

"So what are you wearing?" Mionne asked her, smiling broadly.

"This is a big mistake, I just know it is." Cienna said. But then she asked herself the same question.

Keith pulled up in front of the two-story brown-stone on East Nineteenth Street. He paused a moment after parking his Lexus in front of her door. This was it; this was what he had been waiting all week for. Time alone with Cienna, without work, without the phones, without any distractions. This would tell him how interested he truly was in her. Maybe it would also quash his misgivings about getting involved with her.

Of course, there were many. There were pros and cons to every situation and he had carefully weighed them as he got dressed. The pros had won, hands-down. She was beautiful, sexy, intelligent and independent; qualities he wanted in a woman—qualities he wanted in a wife. Where had that thought come from? He rested his forehead on the steering wheel and concentrated on the here and now. The future would take care of itself.

After a few more minutes, he got out of the car and walked up the steps. Her name was scribbled on a slip of white paper next to the black button that would ring the second-floor apartment. He took a deep breath and pushed the button.

Her voice traveled down to him. "Yes?"

"Hi, it's me. Keith." His voice was a little uneasy.

"Come on up." Cienna rang the buzzer and heard the clicking sound of the front door opening. She was nervous. She had never been nervous about a date.

Probably because she figured if the guy had asked her out, then he was obviously interested. Hence, there was no cause for her to feel the need to impress him. But this time was different. She didn't feel she needed to impress Keith; no, she was pretty sure she had already done that. This time, she was anxious. Anxious to see where this would lead. Anxious to see what he would do, how he would act. She wanted all the answers to her questions right now. She didn't want to wait until the end of the night, the next day or even the next month to see what the future held for them.

Suddenly, her mind drifted back to Bobby. They had met while she clerked in the State's Attorney's office. He worked for the sheriff's department, so she'd see him on her trips to the courtroom with her boss. Casual, polite conversation had quickly led to extended lunches, flowers and then dinners. Dinners and flowers had led to overnights and long weekends. And all of that had led to her losing her job and the sting of first time heartbreak. She was sure she didn't want to go through that again.

Nevertheless, her stomach roiled and bubbled in excited anticipation. She was going out with Keith Page. He had plenty of other women interested in him; she knew a few of them personally. But he had asked *her* out. She was almost amazed.

She nearly jumped out of her skin when he knocked on the door. He was only a foot away, and already she could feel him, the heat he brought with him whenever he came near her, the sexuality that all but oozed out of his pores. She braced herself and opened the door.

Nothing could have prepared him for the sight of her. She literally took his breath away. Thick curls bounced and framed her perfectly round face. Her eyes were shadowed with dark eyeliner and gray eye shadow; her full lips were softly coated with a frosty type of gloss, and when she smiled, he felt the blood quickly rushing from his head to parts in the middle region of his body.

"Hi. I see you found it without any problem." She tried to speak louder than the thumping of her heart. She was sure he could hear, because it drummed in her ears. "Come on in." She moved to the side to let him in. As he brushed past her, she smelled his cologne; all man, all sex, all Keith. She felt a little dizzy but quickly recovered.

He wore casual blue slacks and a really nice, really expensive cream silk shirt. He walked in long, smooth strides as he perused her apartment.

"You have a great view." He looked through the windows, which were covered by sheer mini blinds.

"Yeah, you should see it on New Year's. I don't have to leave my living room." She closed the door behind her.

"I can imagine." He put his hands in his pockets and turned to see her staring at him. She wore black and gold pants with a tiny, checkered print and a gold blouse that wrapped across her breasts and tied at her hip. "So," he cleared his throat that was now dry as toast, "I figured a movie and dinner. What do you think?"

"That sounds good to me," she agreed. "What do you want to see?"

"I'll let you pick."

"Okay, let me see," she said, pretending to think. She knew what she wanted to see. In fact, she and Mionne were supposed to see it tomorrow night. "*Two Can Play That Game*. Is that okay with you?"

"You mean the one with Chestnut and Vivica?"

"Yeah. It looks like it'd be a good eye-opener."

"No, it looks like another man-bashing chick flick. But that's fine." Rolling his eyes, he resigned himself to two hours of sexist torture.

"Well, men do need bashing sometimes. Let me get my purse, and I'll be ready." Though she felt a little more at ease as she walked into her bedroom, her stomach was still doing somersaults, and a low burning had begun between her legs. A nice romantic comedy would be a good diversion.

CHAPTER EIGHT

"That's exactly what women do. As soon as they think they've caught a man doing something he shouldn't, instead of just addressing that issue, they try and get revenge," Keith announced. They had just left the movie and were in his car on their way to the restaurant.

"That's not true. But if the man insists on cheatin' and then lyin' about it, some form of retribution is called for," Cienna argued as they continued to discuss the movie.

"Come on now, she could have just approached him, listened to his side of the story and let it be done. She didn't have to keep the ball rolling."

"How about him plotting the lie from the time he was caught? That's what men do. They think of the lie early on and rehearse it over and over again until they get it right. Bottom line, he shouldn't have been there with another woman."

"The man said it was business," Keith said. Then he had to laugh at the poor lie himself. "You know what they say: It's hard to teach an old dog new tricks."

"Yeah, a leopard never changes his spots either."

"So you're into the monogamy thing, huh?"

"Aren't you?" She was serious now. His views on relationships mattered to her. Even though she refused to admit that this was going to get that far, it was still beneficial to know.

"I guess. I mean, I haven't really had the opportunity to devote myself to one woman for a long period of time, so I couldn't say what I'm into." The car got quiet as they both decided not to explore that topic any further.

"Where are we going now?" Cienna asked.

"I thought we'd get something simple to eat. Have you ever been to Café Centro?" he asked as he made a right turn onto Forty-Seventh Street.

"Yeah, it's in the MetLife Building right?"

"Yeah, that's the one. Does that sound okay to you?"

"Sounds fine. I'm starving."

"Good, 'cause I am, too."

Shortly after, they were seated at a table in the corner. Cienna eased into the comfortable armed chairs and settled in to peruse the menu. It was busy tonight, and the air buzzed with conversation and the clanking of dishes.

"So what do you think?" Keith asked, motioning towards the menu.

"I don't know. Mussels and grilled rabbit aren't high on my list of favorites."

"I know. No soul food in here. Skip down to 'From the Grill.' Maybe you'll find something you like there," he suggested. "Grilled chicken, maybe?"

"No, I'd rather have steak. The T-bone, I guess. Have you had it? Is it good?" Waiting for his response, she shifted slightly in her chair.

"Yeah, they cook it just right. I like mine well done. How about you?"

"Absolutely. I don't want any blood on my plate."

"Okay, so how about we get the three pound T-bone and fries? We can share." He waited for her reply.

"Why? Don't you have enough money to pay for both of us to get our own food?" Cienna asked sarcastically.

"Very funny. Of course I do. I just thought it would be romantic to literally share a meal with you." His eyes sent her a smoldering gaze over the top of the menu.

"I'll just bet you do." She quickly returned her attention to the matter at hand. "At any rate, that sounds good."

"I'm going to start with the mixed green salad."

"You go right ahead. I don't eat salad."

"What? A woman that doesn't eat salad? That's different."

"I'm different," she said as she closed her menu.

"I'm beginning to realize that."

When their food arrived, Keith instinctively began to cut the meat for her.

"I could have done that myself, you know." She smiled at his considerateness.

"I'm sure you could have, but I wanted to do it for you." As he took his first bite, he watched her pour ketchup into a large puddle on the side of her plate and begin dipping her French fries into it. "So tell me about yourself. Not the professional part, I know all that. I want to know about you, the woman."

"There's not much to tell. I'm an only child. My parents live in Brooklyn. My mother's retired and my father works for the post office. I have dinner with them on Monday nights, and I go to church with them on Sunday mornings. That's it in a nutshell."

"You don't go out? What about your girlfriends?"

"Girlfriends have always been hard to come by for me. Too much drama. But Mionne and I are pretty close. We go out sometimes."

"You don't hang out with Reka?"

"Definitely not! Reka talks too much. We went to happy hour a couple of times, and she about drove me up a wall. She's restricted to the office. I did go to lunch with her the other day. I swear, that girl's life is the hottest soap opera in town." Cienna drank from her glass of water. "So what about you? What do you do for fun?"

"I play basketball with a few college buddies on Saturdays and generally work Sunday through Friday."

"Except for when you have a date." *Why had she said that?* She regretted the words the moment they were out of her mouth. But she was curious about the woman who couldn't let him go.

"Yeah, here and there. Do you date much?" Dismissing the casual opening for him to discuss Tyra, he expertly turned the tables.

"Not really. I mean, when a guy I like approaches me, I'll go out with him. We may go out a couple of times, and then something happens and we don't see each other again."

"I'm curious as to what happens." She knew what he was asking and figured there was no use beating around the bush.

"If I decide the guy's worth it, I sleep with him, but then he changes. He gets all protective and territorial and wants to make up all these rules. I just don't have the time or the energy to keep up with all that stuff," she lied.

"So you just want a casual sexual relationship?"

"Sometimes." She shrugged her shoulders, not really wanting to carry this discussion any further.

"What about other times?" Keith watched her dodge his prying eyes.

"I haven't had any other times," she said quietly, then stuck another small morsel of steak into her mouth. He had been right; they did cook it to perfection. It was nice and tender and done all the way through, just the way she liked it.

"Is that kind of relationship enough for you?" He figured there was more to the story than she was offering.

"It has been so far. What about you?"

"I guess we're similar in that regard, too. I haven't really taken the time to settle down and explore a serious relationship with a woman. I guess I'm too focused on the professional aspect of my life."

"I know. See, I have all these things I want to do professionally and it's like, how can I do this and dedicate myself to a relationship at the same time? When I do something; I go all the way, with guns blazing."

Her eyes danced as she discussed her goals. Keith was amazed at how quickly she'd changed. Just a moment ago she'd been sullen, not really wanting to talk, and in the blink of an eye she'd perked right up. He surmised that she didn't want to talk about her past relationships but thought work was a safe subject. However, Keith didn't want to play it safe.

"Yeah, I know, that's how I look at it. But I have to admit that I'm getting tired. I mean, sometimes I think I'd just like to know there's someone there for me who knows me. Someone who knows what I need and when I need it. You can't get that from a fling."

"I guess you're right."

Keith reached across the table to take Cienna's free hand before saying, "Do you know what I need, Cienna?"

Her heart skipped a beat, and she answered honestly.

"I think you need a woman who is time enough for you. Someone who's on your level both mentally and physically. In addition to being just as smart as you are, she would need to be just as ambitious. That way, she would solidly support your dreams as well as chase her own. But she also has to know where to touch you when you're stressed and what to say to you when you're discouraged. Am I right?" They sat perfectly still. In the crowded room, no one existed but them.

"Exactly." His hand moved to massage her wrist. He was getting the distinct impression that she had just described herself. "Do you know what you need?"

"Do you?" Because she didn't know, she asked and waited expectantly for his reply.

He could feel her pulse quicken. "You need a man to treat you as his equal but who knows when to pull your chair out for you or open your car door; a man who'll listen to you with interest and respond intelligently; a man who'll see you've had a hard day and run you a nice hot bath and then come in to wash your back. He has to be able to touch you in all the right places and kiss you until you're limp in his arms. Isn't that what you need, Cienna?"

Because he was too close to the truth, because his touch was making her dizzy, she took a deep steadying breath before replying. "I hadn't really thought of it that way, but I guess that would be nice." She stammered over the words. "I don't think I'm hungry anymore." She snatched her hand away from his and placed it in her lap.

Keith walked her to her door and waited for her to decide if she would invite him in.

Cienna knew if she let him in, the dam that barely held back the flood of emotions about to erupt inside her would burst. So she placed her back against the door and turned to face him.

"Thanks for tonight. I had a good time." She stared up at him. He stood only inches away from her, amusement in his eyes.

"So did I." He figured she had decided not to let him in, which he thought was best because he didn't know if he could control himself any longer. He'd get the goodnight kiss over with and then go home and take a very, very cold shower.

When he took a half-step forward, he felt her breasts rub against his ribs. Her head was directly under his chin, and he placed a finger on her jaw to lift her face to his.

"I've wondered for a while now what you would taste like." His lips were a whisper away from hers.

"It may not be what you expect," she responded softly.

"I've imagined you taste sweeter than chocolate, more arousing than oysters and as potent as a shot of vodka." He brushed his lips against hers, just a light flicker, and felt shivers run down his spine.

"All that, huh? I hope you don't regret this." Cienna lifted her hands to rest on his chest and positioned herself to more comfortably receive his kiss.

"There are no regrets for what should be." His tongue grazed her bottom lip slowly. Cienna opened her mouth, eager to take what he offered. He curled the tip of his tongue and gently lifted her upper lip. Cienna moaned, leaning closer into his embrace.

He suckled her lips, giving them ample attention before coercing her to join in the assault. His tongue stroked hers, quickly, in and out.

Cienna sighed, intrigued. Her eyes fluttered, and she folded her arms around his neck, drawing him closer.

Her tongue snaked out, welcoming him, and a smooth, mellow dance began. Gentle strokes, soft moans and languid movements held them suspended in time.

Keith shifted the angle of the kiss, and Cienna felt herself falling into a bottomless pit of pleasure. His hands roamed recklessly up and down her back, and he gripped her hair to tilt her head back for enhanced access.

Cienna broke the contact, knowing that if she didn't, he wouldn't. He lowered his forehead until it touched hers as they both caught their breath.

"No regrets?" he said.

"No regrets," she answered.

CHAPTER NINE

Keith sat in his office, the cool leather of his chair giving to accommodate his weight as he shifted and turned. He had positioned himself so that he stared out the window. A view of New York's skyline stretched out before him. His mind wasn't on work this morning; no, he had more pleasurable things to think about.

The kiss with Cienna, for example. He had replayed it in his mind over and over all weekend long. More sure than ever now that he wanted to be with her, he had been tempted to call her all weekend, but didn't want to seem too eager. He just had to crack that shell that she had so decisively built around her heart.

It shocked him that it was not a relationship gone bad in her past that made her feel the way she did, at least not one that he knew about. But ambition was enough to cloud anyone's mind. He knew that himself. Amazingly enough, though, he hadn't thought about his own professional goals at all this weekend. He was so engrossed with thoughts of Cienna, it was almost as if the road to being a judge had taken a back seat.

A light tapping on his door had him turning in his chair to stare at Cienna. Her hair was up in a twist now, and her black dress hung loosely over her hips. She was a vision—a stunning vision. His heart thumped and tumbled in his chest. He couldn't find the words to speak, and he hoped he didn't look as stupid as he felt.

"Hey, I hope I'm not disturbing you," she said before stepping into his office.

"No, no, not at all. What's up?" He tried to keep his voice casual.

"I just got a call from Simms. He wants to meet this afternoon. I told him yes, but I wanted to make sure you were available." She didn't take a seat but stood a few inches away from his desk clasping her hands behind her back.

"Ah, no, not really." He was looking at his calendar now. "I have a hearing at one, and I'm almost positive I won't be finished before three. What time are you meeting with him?"

"I told him one-thirty. But I'll call and cancel. What would be a better time for you?"

"No, don't cancel. Why don't you go and meet with him, and then you can brief me over dinner tonight." He hoped she'd agree.

"As much as I might like that idea, I can't. I have dinner with my parents on Mondays. But if you're sure about me going to the meeting alone, I can brief you in the morning." She felt herself swaying now and had to concentrate to stop. She had been really nervous about seeing him again for the first time since their kiss, but when she'd tried to page him, his line was busy. So, she'd opted to come to his office. She was beginning to realize that was a bad decision. She was definitely not ready for this confrontation.

"Oh, yeah. I forgot. Okay, meet with him, and we'll go to lunch tomorrow and talk about it." He watched her fidget.

"We don't have to go to lunch to talk about it. We could just meet in the office. I mean, it is business." She saw disappointment flicker in his eyes. "Besides, I'd kind of like to keep our personal, personal; and our business, business. You know what I mean?" she asked meekly. She was disgusted with herself as the sound of her subdued voice echoed in her ears.

"I guess you're right." He walked around her to close the door. "So personally, how are you?" He sat down on the edge of his desk.

"I'm good. How about you?" She looked directly at him.

"I'm good," he responded, for lack of anything better to say. He really wanted to hold her again.

"Good. I have to go now. I'll buzz you in the morning for a time to meet." She started to walk toward the door, but he stepped in her path.

"I have something for you before you leave." He took her hand and pulled her toward him.

"Oh, really?" She was so confused. One minute, she couldn't wait to see him, and the next minute, she couldn't wait to get away from him. Now, all she wanted was to touch him. He was driving her crazy.

"Close your eyes," he whispered.

"What?" she smiled.

"Just do it. Trust me." When her eyes fluttered shut, Keith placed a fingertip to her bottom lip and traced her soft skin. After a few traces, her supple tongue came out to briefly touch the tip of his finger. His body was instantly alert as he closed his eyes to the sensation.

Cienna continued to suckle his finger. Keith felt the heat from her tongue spreading quickly throughout his body.

"Oh, yeah. Suck it. Suck it," he whispered.

Cienna opened her eyes to see that his were closed; his lips were slightly parted as he concentrated on the sweetness of the moment.

Abruptly, he replaced his finger with his tongue. His lips covered her mouth, feasting on her succulent lips. His free hand lightly grazed her breast until he could feel one agreeable nipple pucker beneath his palm.

"That feels so good," she whispered against his lips.

"I have to have you, Cienna. Soon." His voice was ragged and strained.

"This is crazy," she said through the haze that filled her brain.

"No, being without you is crazy. Tell me you don't like it." Full lips grazed her earlobes.

"I can't." Her breath was coming in small pants now as she held on to his shoulders. "So when can I have you? I need you," he was saying.

"I...I...I can't do this." She tried to pull away. "I'm sorry, I just can't do this right now." She watched a dazed and confused look cross his elegantly cut face.

"It's just a matter of time. You can't run from what you know you want." His eyes held hers in a smoldering gaze. "And you definitely want it. Despite what your mouth says, your body tells me something totally different." He released her from his hold and backed up until he sat on the edge of his desk. His arousal strained against the material of his pants. He felt it throbbing, almost aching with wanting her. He knew she had felt it, too.

"It doesn't matter," she whispered. But she couldn't keep her eyes off him, his hands, and his...How long would she continue to deny the truth?

"You can't even stop looking at it. But it's okay. It'll be here waiting for you. Whenever you're ready to take it, it'll be ready." He stared at her while she continued to stare at his hardness.

"I'll call you." She turned to walk out the door.

"Cienna?" he called to her before she made it completely through the door. "No regrets?"

"No regrets," she said as she smiled at him. It was going to be hard to keep personal, personal, she thought as she walked back to her office.

Keith had no intention of keeping personal, personal. He wanted to be with her, and he would and he wouldn't hide it once he had achieved that feat.

Mionne had wasted her whole lunch hour waiting for Lee at the little café on the corner. He didn't show up, and he didn't call her cell phone to tell her that he wasn't coming. She was getting tired of his bullshit. But she feared she was in love with him. And that meant she would continue taking whatever he dished out.

Lee was the key to saving her from her past. He was going to marry her, buy her a house, and treat her as she deserved to be treated. She stepped off the elevator and walked towards Lee's office. The receptionist stopped her.

"He's at lunch." The girl barely looked up from her magazine. Mionne figured she'd seen her when she first came through the double-doors of the office.

"What time do you expect him?" Mionne gave the receptionist the same barely tolerant attitude the woman gave her on every occasion she'd visited the office.

"He should be back shortly." The girl licked her finger and turned the next page in the magazine she seemed to be so engrossed in.

"Fine," Mionne snapped. "Just tell him I stopped by." She didn't bother to wait for further acknowledgement before heading toward the elevator.

Supremely ticked off, Mionne slammed her palm against the down button. Her mind was racing. Where was he? Who was he with? She knew there was somebody else; she could feel it. A couple of minutes passed, and the elevator still didn't come. Mionne tapped her feet against the carpeted floor and checked her watch for the time. Great, now she was going to be late returning from lunch. Charles would surely jump all over that.

Deciding she'd waited long enough, she walked to the other end of the hall where the service elevators were and pressed the button. She didn't mind being in a less pretty elevator that didn't stop on every floor. No, she didn't mind that at all.

In less than two minutes, the bell sounded, and the elevator doors swung open. Mionne breathed a sigh of relief and took a step to enter the elevator but stopped abruptly when her eyes locked on a familiar face. Her jaw dropped, and her blood pressure rose as she stared at Lee standing against the back wall of the elevator with a skinny blonde draped over him. One long sleek leg was strategically placed between his gapped legs while her tongue snaked in and out of his ear.

At first, Lee didn't move. How could he? The woman was twined around him too tightly. He stared at Mionne in shock before putting his hands around the woman's waist and pushing her away from him.

The woman made a mewling sound before turning to see Mionne standing there. "Oops," she giggled. A hand with red fingernails came up to her mouth in surprise.

"Am I interrupting something?" Mionne asked, barely masking her anger.

"Mionne!" Lee was shocked to see her there of all places. He moved away from the wall when the woman finally disentangled herself from him, but when Mionne moved a step closer, he took two protective steps back.

"Miss, would you please excuse us?" Mionne asked, her voice clipped.

"No, my date and I…"

Mionne cut the woman off with one ice-cold glare that told her she wasn't interested in anything she had to say. "You and your date are finished!"

The woman didn't wait for further instruction as Lee remained quiet in the corner. She stepped off the elevator as quickly as she could.

When they were alone in the elevator, Mionne pushed the button to close the doors.

"Well?" She turned to face Lee.

"Well, what?" Lee thrust his hands into his pockets.

"Who was she? And why were you with her when you were supposed to be at lunch with me?" she demanded.

"She's nobody. I met her at a charity function." He shrugged.

"So she was performing some act of charity for you?" Mionne fumed.

"No, I took her to lunch."

"You were supposed to be taking me to lunch." Her bottom lip quivered as she struggled not to cry.

"She's on the Board of Communications." Lee leaned against the back of the elevator as if he were bored with this whole scene.

"And?"

"And she has a lot of pull with the governor's office. You know I'm working on this deal."

"I know damn well about the deal you're working on. So you'll sleep with her to get her support? Is that it?" Images of Lee and that woman sleeping together raced through her mind.

"This is silly, I have to get back to work." Lee moved around her and reached for the button that would open the door.

"So what about us?" she asked.

"What about us?" He turned back to face her before pushing the button. When she didn't answer, he sighed, clearly annoyed. "Look, we had some fun. You're a terrific woman, and I'd like you to keep working for the company, and I wouldn't mind seeing you again sometime. But right now, I have to concentrate on this deal."

"Just like that?" her voice squeaked.

"Oh, come on, don't tell me you thought this was going somewhere? You know I'm married," Lee complained.

"But you said...," she began.

"No! I never made you any promises." He cut her off, his voice cold and insincere. He pressed his finger against the button quickly. When the doors opened, he turned to her one last time. "I should have listened to my boy, he warned me about you." Lee sighed. "On second thought, I don't think it's such a good idea for us to get together again. I'll have Rachel call you about your next assignment." With that said, he stepped off the elevator and never looked back.

Mionne sank against the wall and watched as Lee walked away from her and the elevator doors closed. She didn't remember pushing the button to go down, but the elevator began to move, and hot tears streaked her cheeks.

CHAPTER TEN

Cienna sat in the lobby waiting for Simms, who, by a quick check of her watch, was about fifteen minutes late for their meeting. His receptionist had told her he was on an overseas conference call, but Cienna couldn't help thinking that he was back in his office doing Lord-knew-what with the woman she'd seen leaving the other day.

She tapped her foot against the stone gray carpet, a sure sign she was becoming irritated. Simms obviously didn't realize that he was not her only client. As important as this case seemed to be to Charles, she had other ones that deserved her time and attention, too. Besides, she'd told her mother she would pick up some fresh bread for dinner tonight—which meant she'd be taking another route entirely that would add an additional twenty minutes to the trip to her parents' home in Brooklyn.

"Ms. Turner, he's ready for you now," the gold tooth-sporting receptionist said to her.

"Thanks." Cienna walked through the door that would lead to his office. She hesitated briefly, remembering her last time here, before knocking on his door.

"Come on in," he yelled from the other side.

"Good afternoon, Mr. Simms," Cienna said. She walked across the burgundy carpet to the heavy oak chairs across from his desk.

"How are you, Ms. Turner?" he asked her.

"I'm fine. The first thing I'd like to discuss is Mr. Barber. What exactly was his position here, and who hired him?" She reached into her briefcase and pulled out a legal pad and a pen.

"You would have to talk to Human Resources about that. They'd have all that information. Anyway, I called you here today because I needed to see you again," he said.

He seemed short of breath, and Cienna wondered if he suffered from some respiratory condition. "I understand. We really need to get on the ball with this. My partner and I were thinking we should probably depose Mr. Barber as soon as possible. The other two claimants don't have as strong a claim as he does, so we'll start with him."

Simms got out of his chair and moved to sit on the edge of his desk. His stomach was significantly larger than she'd first assumed, and she thought he could stand to lose forty or fifty pounds. She wondered how he could even find his penis, let alone be ready to stick it into the first person who came into his office.

Now that he was closer, a sense of familiarity clicked in her mind again. She could have sworn she'd seen him somewhere before—somewhere other than the newspapers or television.

"You're a very pretty woman, Ms. Turner. May I call you 'Cienna'?" he asked.

"No, Ms. Turner will do just fine," Cienna said. She didn't like the way he was looking at her. She quickly uncrossed her legs and clamped them shut in a protective motion.

"You don't remember me, do you?" His eyes narrowed as he watched her trying to figure out from where she knew him. He'd known her the second she had come into his office the other day.

Cienna looked at him closely, still trying to place his face. "Should I remember you?" she asked.

He chuckled. "Club Horizon. About four weeks ago. You were there with your friend when I…"

Memories of the dark club came flooding back. She and Mionne had gone to Club Horizon one Saturday night. They had both been bored and date-less, so Mionne had suggested the club.

Cienna had vehemently argued against it, thinking it would be like the places she'd gone in college. Loud music, excessive drinking, rude people, fights ensuing afterwards; that was not the type of evening she had in mind. But Mionne had argued that this was a classy club with a two-drink minimum, light club music, no rap, and a strict dress code, which normally kept out the riffraff.

Another deterrent was that the club was in Manhattan. Mionne had thought Manhattan would be the selling point for Cienna, but instead Cienna had felt it was a little too far to travel for a couple of drinks and a little dancing.

Finally, after an hour-long debate, Cienna gave in, got dressed and headed out to pick Mionne up. By the time they arrived at the club, Cienna had calmed down considerably. Then after her first drink, she was feeling mellow and relaxed.

The evening had been shaping up just fine until Mionne got onto the dance floor for the millionth time, leaving Cienna at the table alone. Not that she was nervous about being alone; Mionne had been dancing all night, so she'd spent most of the evening alone. But this time an arrogant male decided to join her.

He had slid his paunchy body into her booth, smiling as if he knew something she didn't. "I had to come and see you close up. I thought the booze had muddled my eyesight because from across the room, you looked like the most beautiful woman I'd ever seen. But close up," he sighed, "well, close up, you quite simply *are* the most beautiful woman I've ever seen."

"How many times have you recited that little speech tonight?" Cienna asked. Clearly, his opening line had been rehearsed. He'd known just when to lower his voice, lick his lips and sigh as if truly amazed. Cienna had been instantly turned off.

"That depends." He lifted his eyebrows, giving her a silly grin.

"On what?"

"On how many other beautiful women you see in here." His smile broadened, and he reached for her hand. She moved it just out of his reach.

"That's precisely what I thought." Cienna lifted her drink to her lips and wished he'd go away.

"Do you have a name, pretty lady?"

"I do." She put her glass down and reached for a napkin. That proved to be a mistake, because he took the opportunity to snag her hand up.

"Do I have to guess?" He rubbed his thumb across her knuckles.

"No," she answered tightly and tried to pull her hand away. She didn't like the way he was looking at her, as if he were undressing her with his eyes. And he kept licking his lips, which had begun to repulse her.

"Then how will I know what to call you?"

"You won't, because you won't be calling me." She tugged on her hand again. This time, he smiled and lifted it to his mouth, kissing first her palm, then turning her hand over to kiss the back.

That was it! She'd had enough. With all her strength, she pulled her hand out of his grasp and stood to leave.

"Damn baby, you got back!" he exclaimed as she walked away. "How 'bout you break a brotha off a piece. You got more than enough to share." His voice was slurred. Obviously, he had drunk his fill for the evening.

"How about you go to hell?" she yelled back at him over her shoulder.

She searched the club for Mionne. This was exactly the type of situation she had been afraid of. Her temples pulsated with the headache that was developing. She found Mionne at the bar downing another gin and juice and told her she was leaving.

A few minutes later, Mionne followed her out of the club. They didn't speak at all on the ride home. Cienna was full of disgust over the scene that had just played out, and she assumed that Mionne was about to pass into a drunken stupor.

Now, she realized the man in front of her, the Chief Executive Officer of a highly rated communications firm, was the same man who had clearly harassed her on a prior occasion. And she had to defend him.

Cienna shook her head in an attempt to clear her thoughts. This was business, she reminded herself. What had happened between them happened before she'd been hired to defend him. So she'd put that behind them and start over.

In a business-like voice, she said, "Okay, well, now that we know where we recognize each other from, we can move on." She took a deep breath and lifted her pen to write. "So, when did you first meet Mr. Barber?"

"It doesn't really matter. I'm not gay, and I have more than a dozen women who can attest to that, including my wife. So his allegations are false, and that's that," he said, rubbing a fat hand over his bearded chin. "Let's talk about something else."

"Fine, let's discuss the date in question, April thirteenth." Cienna flipped through notes she'd jotted down earlier. "Were you alone with Mr. Barber in this office?"

"Cienna," he began.

"Ms. Turner," she corrected.

He smiled. "Okay, Ms. Turner, I'm alone in my office with lots of people all the time. Does that mean I'm harassing all of them? Am I harassing you?" His eyebrows raised, and the too-smooth smile spread across his face.

No, he wasn't harassing her at the moment, but he was certainly making her feel uncomfortable. "I am not your accuser, Mr. Simms, and I would appreciate it if you would respond to my questions with an answer rather than an additional question. Now, were you alone with Mr. Barber on April thirteenth?"

"Yes, I was. He works in the IT Department. There was an opening in that department for supervisor, and we were discussing the possibility of him taking that position." He spoke quickly, then waved his hand as if being finished with that topic. "I remembered you as soon as I saw you the other day, but I couldn't say anything with your friend present." One hand moved to stroke the hair on his chin again as his eyes took in everything about her.

Cienna felt his gaze on her and shivered with repulsion.

"Mr. Simms, let me advise you up front that sexual advances, showing preferences regarding sexual gender and pornographic or vulgar behavior—all are considered sexual harassment. Any and all of those acts are punishable in the State of New York. With that said, I'm going to ask that you not bring up that night at the club, nor try to pick up where we left off. I'm your attorney now and would appreciate you respecting that."

"You're a damned fine attorney, too," he told her. "Or so I've heard from Charles," he added quickly.

"Yes, I am. Now can we work on Mr. Barber? As I stated before, we'd like to depose him, so I need some answers from you first."

"I'd rather work on our relationship." His thick tongue snaked out and glided slowly over his lips.

"Okay," Cienna replied. Slapping her pen against the legal pad she held on her lap, she slid both of them into her briefcase and stood to leave. "I can see this isn't going to work. Maybe you'll be more amenable to answering questions when my colleague is present."

When she stood, he stood. They were face-to-face, close enough for him to grab her. But he didn't. "I just meant if you would relax, maybe I could relax and we could get on with the case." He shrugged innocently.

His eyes pinned her to that spot, and she couldn't move.

"At any rate, I'd feel more comfortable meeting with you with my colleague present." Cienna turned and walked toward the door, knowing he was watching her, hating the way that made her feel.

"I'll be in touch with your secretary," she told him from the doorway.

"Just so long as you stay in touch."

Cienna's legs had never moved so fast as they did then. She disregarded the receptionist and three other people standing in the lobby on her flight for the elevators.

The ride back was a blur. Once she was inside the building, Cienna went straight to her office and closed the door. She laid her head on her desk and tried to swallow the bile that rose in her throat.

What was she going to do now? Had Simms harassed her? Had she overreacted? Should she tell Charles? What would he say? She wondered if Simms had called Charles himself and told him Lord-only-knew what. She realized suddenly that she wanted to tell Keith first. She needed to tell him first. Then maybe he could tell her what to do.

Suddenly, a brisk knock sounded, and she nearly jumped out of her chair. She grabbed a tissue and quickly wiped her face. In her anger, she had begun to cry. *Just like a woman,* she thought briefly.

"Come in," she said in a voice that still sounded a bit shaky.

"You got a minute?" Mionne asked quietly.

Cienna could see that Mionne looked a little weary, too. So she gestured for her to come in. "Close the door."

"I just need to talk to somebody," Mionne started. "Are you okay?" she asked, noting Cienna's appearance.

"Yeah, I'm fine. I think it's my allergies or something. Now, what's on your mind?" Cienna sniffled and put the tissue in the trashcan.

"Man troubles."

"Oh, Lord, what did Lee do now?" Cienna smiled briefly.

"I caught him with another woman."

"Oh? Oh my, that's not good, is it?" Cienna noted that Mionne looked as if she were going to crumble at any moment. "What did you do?"

"I caught them, and then I got him by himself. But then I just couldn't...I didn't know what to say. I said some things, but it didn't feel like enough. I think I should have said some other things, but I just couldn't think. So I just walked away. I guess I was stupid for thinking he was in love with me." Tears quietly rolled down her cheeks.

"No, you weren't stupid. You believed what he told you because that's what you wanted to believe. He's the fool, and don't you let him make you think otherwise." Cienna came around the desk to take the chair next to Mionne. She grabbed her friend's hand in an effort to console her.

Hadn't she been in that same position seven years ago? Hadn't Bobby done the same thing to her? It had taken her almost a year to find out that he'd been playing her for a fool. He'd been sleeping with her and with several other women in the courthouse at the same time. She remembered how embarrassed and ashamed she'd been when she found out.

And, of course, he'd lied at first—denying the undeniable. Then he'd shifted the tables and made it her fault. She wasn't adventurous enough, she wasn't sexy enough, and, oh, she didn't want to do the things that other women were willing to do. She'd been devastated. Her whole world had been a lie, and the truth crushed her.

Now she watched her friend experiencing the same feelings, and her heart went out to her.

"But maybe I wasn't good enough for him. Maybe I did nag him too much. You know, he said one day last week, I was just as bad as his mother with my nagging and whining." Mionne had begun to shake.

"Come on now, don't do that. You've been a good woman to him. You've given him everything you possibly could. He should've been kissin' the ground you walk on." Cienna felt herself becoming angry with the whole male population. Why was it always the woman's fault that the man was a dog?

"Listen, Mionne, you know what you want, and you've got a right to love somebody who will be anything and everything you want all the time. Don't let him break your heart. He's not worth it." She could say these things now and believe them. Seven years ago, though, she wouldn't have thought any of what she'd just said could be true.

"I know. But it still hurts," Mionne said tremulously.

"I know it does. But think of it this way. It's his loss. You'll find somebody better than him, but he'll never find anyone as good as you."

"You're right. Forget that sorry-ass punk." Mionne wiped away her tears with the back of her hand.

"That's right! You don't need him!" Cienna felt better now that Mionne was coming out of that mushy girl state. "You're stronger than that, let him go. Be done with him. It'll take some time for the hurt to go away, but it will." She knew that for a fact.

"Yeah, and in the meantime, if he comes near me, I'm going to kill him. No, I'm gonna cut off his balls and mail them first-class to that little hussy downstairs. Then, I'm going to kill him."

"Now, Mionne, you know it's not her fault. He's probably lying to her, too." Cienna laughed. "But that would be something if she opened a box and found his balls wrapped in tissue paper." They both laughed at that thought.

CHAPTER ELEVEN

Adelle Turner shuffled around the kitchen preparing her evening meal of baked chicken, mashed potatoes and gravy, and creamed corn, all of Cienna's favorites, which was a good thing after the day she'd had.

"What's on your mind, baby?" Adelle asked. She'd been watching Cienna glaring out the small window above the sink.

"Oh, nothing. I just had a really rough day." The scene with Mionne was still fresh in her mind, and so were the memories it had brought back.

"You wanna talk about it?" Adelle wanted to know what was on the child's mind but she wouldn't push. She'd learned long ago not to push Cienna when she wasn't ready to talk.

"Not really." Cienna shrugged. Children played in the playground across the street. She wished her life could be that carefree again.

"It'll help." Dropping large chunks of butter into the steaming potatoes, Adelle turned her back to Cienna.

"You always say that, Mama."

"And I'm always right, dear." Licking butter off one of her fingers, she began to mash the potatoes.

"A client hit on me today." On a long sigh, Cienna said the words quickly and waited to see if she felt better. She didn't.

"What do you mean, 'hit on you'?" The spoon Adelle held clanked into the pot as she spun around to see her child.

Cienna recited the events of her meeting with Simms and the night in the club. Adelle cursed and fussed and all but got in the car on her way to town to kick Simms' ass for messin' with her baby.

"It's okay, Mama, I'll handle it," she reassured her.

"You better, or else I'll have to make a trip to the city myself." Adelle resumed her vigil over the poultry that simmered in the oven while Cienna went back to watching the kids across the street.

"This guy at work asked me out last week," Cienna volunteered.

"Oh?" Adelle's ears perked up again.

"Umm hmm. We went out on Friday." A little girl kicked the bright yellow ball, and it bounced across the street. "He seems nice enough, but I don't know." Shrugging, she decided the kids were more interesting than her problems with Keith.

"What's his name?" Adelle asked.

"Keith. Keith Page."

"Do you like this Keith?"

"He's okay, I guess." The ball had been returned to its owner and was now being thrown back and forth between the children.

"I take it he likes you if he asked you out."

"Yeah, I guess."

"So what's the problem?" Adelle knew her child well enough to know that something about this man bothered her. She could probably guess what it was, but decided it would be better if Cienna told her.

"Who says there's a problem?" Cienna waited a beat before adding, "I can't get involved with a man at work. For one thing, it's too distracting; I need to be able to focus on my work. And besides, although it's never been said, I just don't think office romances are appropriate."

"Okay, then don't get involved with him."

"But I like him." *And I want him,* she wanted to say but she didn't think Adelle would take well to hearing about her daughter's sexual fantasies about a co-worker.

Cienna finally moved away from the window to sit at the kitchen table. Her fingers outlined the yellow gingham check that decorated the old worn tabletop.

"What do you want to do, Cienna? That's what you need to ask yourself."

"I don't know." Cienna laid her head on the table. "I mean, I don't want to lose my job again, that's for sure."

"You can't keep living in the past, Cienna. What happened with Bobby was a horrible thing, but you got through it. It's time for you to move on." Adelle remembered all too well the time when her daughter's life had been shattered by love.

Cienna felt as if she were stuck in the middle of a whirlwind. So many things were going on in her life right now. This thing with Keith, the case with Simms, Simms' innuendos, Mionne's breakup with Lee. It was all just too much for her to get a grip on at the moment. "I know, but if I get involved with Keith, the same thing could happen again."

Adelle tried to console her only child. "I don't think so. You're not the same person you were all those years ago."

"But a relationship just blurs your priorities." Folding a napkin repeatedly, Cienna tried to sort the flurry of emotions that had been roaring through her for the past few days.

"A real relationship becomes another priority, Cienna. You can have both. Your job and a man." Deftly handling the knife and the conversation, Adelle continued mildly, "If that's what you want."

"He just won't let up. The more I tell him I can't get involved, the more determined he is to prove me wrong." Propping her chin on her hands, she watched her mother.

"That means he's really interested."

"Bobby was really interested in the beginning, too."

"He's not Bobby, Cienna. You can't go through life comparing every man you meet to Bobby. It's not fair to them, and it's not fair to you."

The memory of the worst day of her life reared its ugly head again. This time, she allowed herself to walk down that road again.

She had come home from work about an hour early. They had just wrapped up a really huge homicide case, and Cienna was beat. All she wanted to do was fix something quick to eat and climb into bed.

Inserting her key into the lock, she turned the knob. To her surprise, the door didn't budge. She retracted her key and searched for the funny-shaped one for the top lock, wondering to herself why the top lock would be locked. She knew she hadn't locked it when she left the house that morning, and Bobby was home, she could hear the TV. Not that he would get his lazy ass up to let her in. When the door finally swung open, Bobby was standing directly behind it with a stunned look on his face.

"Damn, you tryin' to knock me down or what?" he said disgustedly.

"Why were you standing by the door? It was obvious you had no intention of opening it for me." She began taking her coat off. Once her coat was on the hanger, she turned to see where Bobby had gone.

He was still standing by the front door. He was truly a silly man, and with each passing day their relationship seemed to dwindle. She wondered briefly what she could do to revive their lackluster connection, but came up blank.

She shook her head and walked towards the bathroom. In a split second, Bobby ran past her to stand in front of the bathroom door.

"Where are you going?"

"To the bathroom. Do you mind?" She wondered why it mattered to him.

"Why don't you change your clothes first? I mean, you usually go in the bedroom and change your clothes first," he said, continuing to block the doorway.

"I have to go to the bathroom. Move out of my way, boy." She tried to push his bony body out of her way. For such a small man, he had a lot of strength.

"What I tell you 'bout callin' me *boy*? You know I don't play that. Call me by my name!" He was yelling now, and Cienna was starting to get pissed herself. Why was he picking a stupid argument with her as soon as she came in? He usually waited until she had cooked dinner to start talkin' stupid, and better still, why wouldn't he let her go to the bathroom? The moment the question entered her mind, the answer became clear.

"Tell your little bitch she can come out now," she said calmly.

"What? What are you talking about?" His feigning stupidity only adding to Cienna's growing suspicions.

"I'm not stupid, she's in the bathroom, and your tired ass is caught again." At that moment, she heard the knob turn and saw the woman standing behind Bobby in her underwear. She should have been shocked, she should have been hurt, but at that moment, she was just tired. Tired of him, tired of the same shit, tired of it all.

What had she done to deserve all this drama in her life? She backed away from the door and watched as Bobby shielded the woman and led her into the bedroom. *Her* bedroom! This was an all-time low, even for him. He had had the balls to sleep with another woman in the bed that he shared with her. She was close to her breaking point.

They both returned from the bedroom and stood at the front door looking as stupid as they should have been feeling. Cienna couldn't even bring herself to look at the woman. She knew that this was the same one, Wanda, from just a month earlier. The one who worked in another department in the courthouse with them.

What was it this woman had that made it impossible for him to stay away from her? She knew the answer to that: There was no commitment, no obligation. She hoped in her heart that he would decide to leave with her, but after the door closed, she heard his footsteps. Had he ever been smart enough to do anything right? She couldn't remember.

"What's for dinner?" he asked casually. She couldn't speak, couldn't move, she almost couldn't breathe. This was not happening again. With the last bit of pride she could muster, Cienna went into the bedroom and began putting his clothes into a trash bag. She should have done this a long time ago. She wondered who was the bigger fool, he or she.

"Where you going?" Bobby asked as he stood in the doorway.

"I'm not going anywhere. The question is, where are you going?" And that was all she said. An hour later, a confused and angry Bobby was picking up the trash bags from the hallway where she had thrown them. Cienna locked the door and put the chain on it, walked over to the couch and sat down heavily. This had been a long time coming, she knew, but that didn't stop the devastation. Crushed and depleted, she had cried through the night.

Shaking her head at the memory, she refocused on the situation at hand. "I know he's not Bobby. But I keep remembering how things were with him when I'm with Keith."

"Is it the same?" Her mother leaned over to open the oven.

"No. Keith's more mature than Bobby. He's focused. He has goals."

"So what's the real problem?"

"I'm afraid." Out of excuses, Cienna admitted defeat.

"Afraid he'll cheat on you?"

"I'm afraid that all the interest he has now will go away in time, and then he'll decide I'm not what he really wanted in the first place. Isn't that what Bobby did?" She sounded like a little girl. She felt like a little girl sitting in her mother's kitchen, waiting for her to tell her what to do.

"Bobby was a fool. He wanted to have his cake and eat it too. Now, I don't know this Keith fella, but from what you've said about him, he doesn't sound like a fool. Either way, you can't live your life in a cocoon because you're afraid to be hurt. You healed after the last time, and if it happens again, you'll heal again. There are no guarantees, Cienna." Adelle touched her daughter for the first time that afternoon—a gentle caress on her shoulders.

"I know. But you and Daddy are so happy." Relaxing under her mother's touch, Cienna felt her shoulders slump.

"Yeah, it took me years to train that man, and he still ain't right." They both laughed. Kissing her daughter on the forehead, Adelle went back to her meal.

Cienna sat at the table thinking of what her mother had just said. Surprisingly enough, she did feel better after talking about it. She still didn't know what to do, but she felt better.

CHAPTER TWELVE

"Hello?" Cienna answered the phone, thinking it was probably Mionne calling for the billionth time. She was having a hard time dealing with the Lee situation. When Cienna got in from dinner with her parents, she'd found her message light blinking furiously. Mionne, who sounded desperate and distraught, had left four messages.

"Hi." It took Cienna two seconds to figure out who it was. "To what do I owe the pleasure of this call?" She was surprised to be hearing from him.

"I wanted to hear your voice," Keith said huskily.

"Oh?" Cienna answered for lack of anything better to say.

"How was your dinner?"

"Same ol', same ol'. Daddy sat in front of the television with a TV tray in front of him, and Mama and I sat in the kitchen talking about everything from church to politics. And how was your evening?"

"Lonely." There was a pause. "I didn't think I'd want to be with you so much, but I guess yesterday was just a tease." He laughed lightly.

"I don't think it was a tease. It was more like a prelude."

"Yeah? I hope so. So how was your meeting with Simms?"

Cienna had almost forgotten about that disaster, she was so happy to be talking to Keith. She had told her mother, and her mother had advised her to tell Charles and let someone else handle the case, and then to sue the bastard herself. But she wasn't quite sure he'd actually crossed the line with his innuendo. However, some of it might be construed as sexual harassment since she had made it perfectly clear that she was not interested in him on a personal level. Still, she hadn't decided what she was going to do. She knew she wanted to tell Keith. She wanted his advice.

"Um, something sort of happened at the meeting that I wanted to tell you about, but I was going to wait until tomorrow."

"What happened?"

"He...I mean, Simms...he ah..." Cienna couldn't find the words. Now she could see how hard it was for victims to tell what had been done to them. A small part of her felt that Keith might blame her. Another part knew that that was preposterous.

"Cienna, what happened? What is it?" Keith demanded. He felt a sense of alarm. Her voice had changed the moment he asked her about Simms. He didn't like the way she sounded now at all.

"Um, he tried to make a pass at me. I mean, I think he was coming on to me." She spoke quickly, then waited for his response, praying it wouldn't be negative.

"He did what? Are you serious?" Keith was screaming into the phone.

"Yes, I'm dead serious. I think that's why he had his secretary call me instead of you." Cienna took a deep breath before continuing. "I met him a few weeks ago when I went to a club with Mionne. I thought he looked a little familiar, but I couldn't place him until today. Anyway, at the club he was drunk and pretty insistent. He grabbed my hand and made lewd comments. To make a long story short, this afternoon he informed me that he remembered me from the club and that he still wanted to get to know me better."

"I am going to kick his fat ass!" Keith said through clenched teeth. "What else happened?"

"Nothing, really. He just evaded questions about the case and kept directing personal remarks at me. It was really creepy." Cienna felt hot tears streaming down her face as she recited the story for the second time today. She absolutely hated crying. It was weak and demeaning, and she'd sworn she would never be either of those things.

"I'll be there in ten minutes." Keith hung up the phone.

Fifteen minutes and a cup of tea later, Cienna pressed the button to let Keith in. She had put on her robe and tied it tightly about her waist. Her hair was up in a ponytail, and she wore no makeup. As she walked to the door, that fact dawned on her, and she silently fussed at herself. Maybe he wouldn't notice.

He came through the door gathering her up into his arms. He held her so tightly she thought he would crush her ribs. "Are you okay?" he asked her once he let her go.

"Yeah, I'm fine. I should've told you it wasn't necessary for you to come over...," she started to say.

"Of course I came," he interrupted. "He upset you, I could hear it in your voice. I wanted to see for myself that you were okay." He walked her over to the couch.

"I am okay," she said, but her bottom lip quivered. "Dammit, now you're going to make me cry again."

"It's okay. You can cry." He pulled her onto his lap and stroked her arms. "It's alright. He violated you. I understand."

"No, I don't think you do. Men don't seem to think that a woman can tell them no. It's just like Matt and all the other guys at the office. I tell them I don't want to go out with them and they just keep trying and trying. Like I'm supposed to want them, I'm supposed to want them to pay attention to me. But I don't. Simms just thinks everybody wants him, whether it's a woman or a man. I just don't understand."

"Not all men have a hard time deciphering the meaning of the word no." He spoke softly, his hands moving gently over her arms.

"Keith, what if I can't work with him anymore?" She hadn't really given that a lot of thought, but Keith's presence reminded her of the case. She wondered what she should do.

"I thought about that all the way over here. Charles isn't going to like it."

"I know. I have to figure out a way to tell him tomorrow. Simms has probably already called him by now complaining because I walked out on our meeting."

"You did the right thing. I'll go with you to talk to Charles."

Cienna thought of going into Charles' office and telling him that Simms had commented on her looks and suggested getting to know her better. She wondered what Charles' response would be. He probably wouldn't respond at all, considering half his male staff had done the same thing to her on prior occasions, sometimes with Charles present. No, that wouldn't make a difference to him. He wouldn't understand.

"You know, I don't think I want to go to Charles just yet."

"Why not?" Keith blinked in confusion.

"Because it's not like he touched me or anything he said was that bad."

"Maybe not, but his comments were inappropriate, and he should know that. I mean, damn, he's already being sued for sexual harassment. How stupid is it to harass your attorney?" Keith had been asking himself that question all the way over to her apartment.

"I know, but this is a really big case. If RES gets this deal with the state, he'll be the sole communications provider throughout New York. He'll be all over the news, and if we can get him off these charges, that would mean more business from him for the firm."

"Cienna, baby, listen to yourself. You're more worried about drumming up business for the firm than standing up to a slime like Simms. You know if he made those remarks to you, it's likely that he harassed those other women and Barber." Keith stared at her. Cienna was silent. "But if you get him off, that will put you in line for partner. Is that it?"

"I know what you're saying is right, but I have a job to do and I'd like to give it another shot. If all of our meetings with Simms are done together, he won't bother me anymore. And if it looks like there's too much evidence against him, which there probably is, then we can propose a reasonable settlement and be done with it. I'm just not ready to throw in the towel yet," she sighed.

Keith stared at her. She was so naturally pretty. Long lashes fanned her skin each time her eyes closed, and her lips beckoned to be kissed. She enticed him without even knowing what she was doing. Reluctantly, he admitted to himself that he would do anything for her. "Okay, if that's the way you want to handle it. But if he makes one more wrong move toward you, you're off this case," he said adamantly. "I mean it, I'll go to Charles myself if I have to," he added when she still didn't respond.

Because Cienna knew he would, she nodded her head in agreement then laid her head on his shoulder, allowing herself to be comforted.

Holding her on his lap, Keith suddenly realized he was in trouble. She was soft and warm and pliant. The way she shifted so that she was even closer to him and the warmth of her breath on his neck had him getting hard. His first instinct was to drop her on the floor and move as far away from her as possible. Now was not the time for him to make moves on her.

But he couldn't let her go. He couldn't break the contact that he was sure would be the death of him.

Cienna had felt the mood change, too. His body was arousing all sorts of emotions in her that she hadn't felt in a long time. Her breasts ached for him to touch them, and she throbbed deep between her legs. She raised her lips and kissed his neck. His sharp intake of breath encouraged her, and she moved to his ear.

Keith tried everything. He thought of baseball, he thought of a cold shower, everything. But nothing would take his mind off her. Her tongue was moving in quick darting motions inside and outside of his ear. Her hands were on the back of his head, moving him to where she wanted him to be. His fingers clenched on her arms and the hand that had been resting on her knee moved up to her thigh.

He turned his head to meet her lips. They stared at each for one second, and then it was over. He took her mouth with quickness. His tongue invaded her mouth, and he sank into her sweetness. She moaned and he gripped her even tighter.

He pushed her back onto the couch and lay on top of her. Her robe fell open just a bit, enough for him to see the swollen mounds beckoning to him. His dark hands moved the smooth material away and cupped the lighter-toned flesh of her breasts. She wet her lips and moaned with delight.

In an instant, his lips were covering the dark nipple and suckling it. Cienna reached down to untie the robe and let it fall open, giving him even more access. He held both her breasts in his hands now. "My God, you are so beautiful," she heard him say in a ragged voice. "So damn beautiful."

He returned his attention to her mouth, but didn't take his hands off her breasts as he kissed her fervently. He kneaded her breasts like mounds of fresh dough, stopping briefly to grasp the nipples between his fingers.

Cienna thought she would scream. Her hands ran madly over his back. She wished he would reposition himself so that she could touch the hardness that was pressed against her thigh. It was that thought that set off alarm bells in her head. What was she doing? She couldn't sleep with him. He was her colleague. This wasn't right. No matter how good it felt, it wasn't right.

"Stop!" She struggled to catch her breath. When Keith looked at her questioningly, she tried to wriggle free of his embrace. "We can't...I can't do this," she said.

Keith used every bit of control he had and mentally recited every word his mother had said about a woman saying no. "Okay. But this is the last time you'll be able to stop me, Cienna." He rose and sat in the chair across from her. It was going to take a minute before he could speak intelligently. He dragged his hands over his face. "My advice to you is until you think you can handle this, don't get close to me, don't touch me, nothing. I can't promise I won't take what I want and ask questions later."

"You'd never do that," she said quietly. "But I'm sorry. I shouldn't have let it get that far. I'm still reeling from yesterday. I should have stopped you from coming over here." Cienna sat up on the sofa and pulled her robe securely around her breasts.

"No, I should've known better. It's not a good time for you right now. I shouldn't have pushed."

"You didn't. I actually started it, and I apologize for that. But we're co-workers, and this is not the smartest thing to do. It might even be against office policy."

Keith looked at her searchingly. "Are you serious?" He asked her. "First of all, Benton and King doesn't have a policy on office relationships, nor do they have any idea what's going on between us."

Cienna interrupted. "Still, I don't think office relationships are appropriate. Look at the trouble Simms is in now."

"Come on, Cienna, this isn't harassment, and it isn't one-sided. We both want this, and we're both consenting adults. It's our business, it has nothing to do with the office."

"But we met at the office, and we do work there together."

"So what? That doesn't mean we can't be involved personally. We're both mature. It's not like we're going to have an argument and go to work the next day throwing things at each other." He was getting angrier with every argument she came up with. He had no idea how close to home that statement had been to Cienna.

"But if we did, who do you think would be the first to lose their job, me or you?" she asked sharply.

"That's ridiculous, Cienna. Nobody's going to lose their job. Where do you get this stuff?" He was amazed that she could come up with all these different scenarios.

"I really don't want to talk about this right now."

"Okay. But we will talk about it. Soon. I'm gonna go now because I can't stay near you another minute and not want to touch you." He rose from his chair and stared down at her. "Walk me to the door, Cienna." He extended his hand to her. Surprisingly, she took it.

They walked to the door in silence. He dropped her hand and held her by the shoulders. "We'll deal with Simms tomorrow, okay?" Cienna nodded her head in agreement.

"And tomorrow night, we're going to have dinner at my place, and we're going to talk about us. Okay?" He was staring at her, and she felt as if his eyes would burn right through her.

"Okay," she said in that meek-ass voice that was becoming all too familiar to her.

He loosened his grip on her shoulders and slowly caressed her back. "Now I'm going to kiss you goodnight," he told her moments before his lips claimed hers in a sweet, gentle kiss that rocked through her body like bolts of lightning. Her arms went up to wrap around his neck, and she stood on tiptoe to increase the contact. The kiss changed. Their tongues dueled in a contest that would not end here, and they both savored the delicious taste of each other.

"I'd better go now." Keith reluctantly broke the contact. "I'll see you tomorrow."

As Cienna stood there for a minute trying to analyze what had happened, she heard Keith call through the door, "Lock the door and go to bed, Cienna."

She smiled and clicked the three locks into place. She waited until she heard his footsteps walking away before she returned to her bedroom.

CHAPTER THIRTEEN

"So you're sure you don't want to talk to Charles yet?" Keith asked her again. She'd already told him that she wanted to try and handle the situation with Simms herself, but he wanted to make absolutely sure this was how she wanted to proceed.

"No, not just yet. I'm going to call Simms and tell him in no uncertain terms that I am not interested in him in any other way besides as a client and that his advances will not be tolerated. That'll probably scare him off." She hoped it would. After Keith had left the previous night, she'd given the situation a lot of thought. This was a really important case, and she didn't want to jeopardize it by running to Charles with complaints. She wasn't going to back down from Simms, nor was she going to bail out of what could be the most important case of her life. No, she was determined to stick it out and see this case through to the end, even if Simms was guilty.

"It's your call. I still think you should let him know what's going on, but I'll support your decision. Just don't go to Simms' office again by yourself." He'd told her all this earlier this morning when he'd stopped by her office to check on her, but he repeated it again. Although he had no desire to be face-to-face with the man, as he didn't know if he'd be able to keep his hands off him, he wasn't about to allow Cienna to face him alone.

"I won't. I'm just going to call him today."

"Let me know how it goes."

"I will."

"Cienna?"

"Yes?"

"I'm really looking forward to tonight."

Cienna sighed at the mention of the evening ahead. Things had changed between them, and the sooner she accepted that, the better off they were going to be. Just how much change she was going to allow at this stage, she wasn't sure, but just as with Simms, she wasn't about to back down from this fight either.

"I am, too. Should I bring anything?" she asked.

"Just yourself," he replied.

"Okay."

"Mr. Simms is out of his office at the moment. I can take a message and harereceptionist, becausee him get back to you."

Cienna knew the voice must belong to the gold-toothed receptionist because she heard gum smacking. "That's fine; could you have him call Cienna Turner please? I'm with Benton and King. He should already have the number."

Hanging up the phone, she opened another one of her files and was preparing to dictate a letter to her secretary when Mionne walked in.

"Hey, girl. How're you today?" Cienna had been closeted in her office all morning, so she hadn't seen anyone else from the office. Mionne took a seat and simply stared at Cienna for a few minutes before answering.

"I don't know what to do. This thing with Lee is really bothering me." Mionne reached into the candy jar that Cienna kept on the end of her desk and unwrapped a Hershey's Kiss™ and plopped the chocolate into her mouth.

Cienna put her Dictaphone down and stared at Mionne. "You're taking this breakup kind of hard, huh?" she asked.

"I thought he was going to marry me," Mionne said when she finished chewing.

"Did he actually say that? I mean, did you two talk about marriage?" Mionne had never mentioned anything to her about marriage, so Cienna was a little shocked at her admission.

"He used to say that we would always be together. Doesn't that mean marriage?"

"No, not really," Cienna replied. The look on Mionne's face told her that was not the response she had been expecting. "To be perfectly honest, I think he's already married."

Mionne remained quiet.

"He is, isn't he?" Cienna asked.

"So what? He said it hasn't been a real marriage for a long time. If he wasn't going to marry me then, why would he have said that?" Mionne asked pointedly.

"He didn't really say anything. I can't believe you've been sleeping with a married man all this time." Though she had suspected it, Cienna was nevertheless upset to have Mionne confirm her suspicion. "You should have known this would never go anywhere, that he would never leave his wife for you. Mionne, they never do."

"No, it wasn't like that with Lee. We had something special. I know we did. Wouldn't you be upset if you found your boyfriend with another woman?"

Would she? Hadn't she? Cienna cringed at the thought. "Yes, Mionne. I would. But Lee wasn't really your boyfriend. He used you, and you let him."

"You mean maybe I wasn't good enough for him to marry? I'm not good enough for anybody to marry, right?" Mionne's voice had changed. Her posture stiffened.

"Look, I didn't say that. I'm sure you'll find somebody who'll want to marry you someday, but Lee is clearly not that someone. For one, he's already married, which puts him in no position to propose marriage to another woman. At least not legally." Cienna was being honest with her friend because that's what she thought Mionne wanted. But the look on Mionne's face was saying something totally different. Cienna was afraid she'd crossed the line.

"You know what, I don't even know why I came in here to talk to you. I should have known you'd take this road." Mionne rolled her eyes.

"And what road is that?" The right one, Cienna thought, but smartly remained quiet.

"The high-and-mighty road you always take with people. Like you never made any mistakes in your perfect little life. Like no man has ever let you down." Mionne was angry, and the sway of her head and tone of her voice stressed that fact.

"I never said I didn't make any mistakes. And, Lord knows, I've had men let me down. But I've tried to learn from those mistakes, to watch out for the signs. But hopping into bed with a married man is a no-win situation. You should have known that going in. Didn't you expect him to cheat on you? After all, he was already cheating on his wife." Mionne wasn't the only one who could cop an attitude.

"Not everybody's as beautiful as you are, Cienna. We can't all have intelligent, rich men on their knees begging to be with us." Mionne's voice dripped with sarcasm that cut Cienna to the bone.

"That's not fair, this isn't about me," Cienna whispered. She'd never flaunted her looks or the fact that men were attracted to her. It hurt her sorely to realize that Mionne felt this way about her, although she shouldn't have been surprised. This was the reason she didn't have any girlfriends. There always seemed to be competition between women, competition that was brutal and unforgiving. Cienna had just fallen victim to it.

"What's not fair? That there was somebody out there that didn't want you; that wanted me instead? Or that I got some, and you're still sitting pretty behind that desk dripping at the panties every time Keith comes near you?" Mionne stood to leave. "Tell me something. Do you think Keith is chasing you around in hope of *marrying* you? Or is it more like he wants to get you into his bed? Because, like it or not, the bottom line is sex! Sex is what keeps men and women together. I may not be beautiful, Cienna, but I do have something going for me, and if it happens to be sex, then that suits me just fine. There's nothing wrong with enjoying sex or sleeping with a man just because you want to. There is, however, something wrong with denying yourself just because you're too scared to try something new, something different, or hell, just to try anything at all!"

"You misunderstood what I was trying to say. All I wanted was for you to consider your part in the downfall of this dysfunctional relationship. I mean, what did you ever get out of it?

Mionne had no intention of trying to justify her nights with Lee. Besides, Cienna wouldn't understand anyway. Some women had to do drastic things to get ahead in this world. Everybody wasn't born with beauty and brains as Cienna had been.

"You know what, it doesn't really matter what I thought or what you think. It's over now, and that's fine. I'll deal with it. But you and your snotty little attitude, I don't have to deal with anymore!" Mionne walked out, slamming the door behind her.

Cienna placed her head between her hands and tried to figure out what had just happened. One minute she thought she was giving her friend advice, and the next she was defending herself against hurtful names and allegations about her personality. What in the world was going on?

"Mr. Simms on line five," Reka announced over the intercom.

Oh Lord, she sighed, *that's all I need right now*.

Scooping up the receiver, she positioned it against her ear and put on her professional voice. "Cienna Turner."

"Hello, beautiful. It's about time you decided to stop beating around the bush."

"Mr. Simms," Cienna interrupted, "I just called you to make one thing perfectly clear. I am your attorney representing you for the same type of inappropriate, behavior you have displayed towards me. I think your comments towards me are inappropriate and I do not welcome or enjoy them. Need I remind you how serious the charges against you are or how serious they are going to become if you continue harassing me? Because, make no mistake about it, I will sue you and run you through the wringer if I have to. Do I make myself perfectly clear?" She was fired up. The scene with Mionne had sparked something within her, something almost violent.

There was silence on the line for all of three seconds before he laughed. "You sure are one feisty little lady, aren't you? Well, that's good, that's just the way I'll need you to be when we get to court. Now, since you brought up the case, let's not forget how much your firm stands to make from my company should things go the right way."

Cienna couldn't believe it. After harassing her, he actually had the audacity to try to intimidate her. "Exactly what are you saying, Mr. Simms?"

"I'm saying that it would be a shame if the time you've spent building your reputation and career came to nothing because of your inability to handle this case." He let the words linger a moment. "Now, I'd like to meet with you on Friday. Is four o'clock okay?"

She got his meaning loud and clear. She'd called to give him her ultimatum, and he'd issued his own to her. "Four is fine," she told him. If she had to suck it up and deal with him to get where she wanted to be, she would, but she was going to give him hell all the way. "My colleague and I will be there." She didn't even give him a chance to respond before she hung up. "Ignorant bastard!" she exclaimed, thankful that the door to her office was closed.

CHAPTER FOURTEEN

Candles and fresh flowers were what his mother had advised for dinner with Cienna. She'd also told him not to push, to let her come to him. But Keith wasn't sure he was going to take that advice. After all, his mother had no idea how stubborn Cienna was.

She'd called twenty minutes ago to say that she was on her way, and he was pacing the floor waiting for her. He was anxious to share his feelings with her and wondered how she would react. He was in love with her; there was no doubt in his mind. Cienna, on the other hand, would almost certainly doubt him. She'd probably get all flustered and recite all the reasons why a relationship between them couldn't possibly work, but he'd planned his rebuttal. He'd simply give her all the reasons why it could work. He was determined to wear her down.

The phone and the doorbell rang simultaneously. He literally stood between them both, wondering which one he should get first. He opted for the phone, figuring he didn't want any interruptions once he was with Cienna.

Snatching the receiver, he all but yelled, "Hello?" He didn't get an answer. He knew who it was. Tyra. She didn't seem to understand that she was crossing the line to harassment by calling him at work and at home numerous times a day. He'd have to make her understand that. He hung up the phone, repeating an unsavory course of expletives before approaching the door.

"Did I interrupt something?" Cienna asked when he snatched the door open.

"Nah, just a crank caller. Come on in."

Once she was in the apartment and Keith had closed the door behind her, she checked the room out. His living room was invitingly decorated in earth tones, from the chocolate brown leather chairs to the plush beige carpet.

"Nice place." She continued a perusal of the African-American portraits hanging on the walls throughout the room. "Did you decorate yourself?" she said, mildly amused.

"Yes, I did. Is there a problem?" He smiled at her questioningly. She wore jeans and a t-shirt that clung to her like a second skin.

"No. No problem. You did a really good job," she answered. "In this room, at least."

"I'm glad you like it. Now come and sit down. Dinner won't be ready for another fifteen or twenty minutes." He sat them down on the couch where his beige khakis and white polo shirt were a sharp contrast to the darkness of the sofa. The Rolex he wore sparkled against his dark skin.

Sitting next to him, Cienna felt a longing that had become familiar to her whenever she was around Keith. "So, what are we having? TV dinners?" She smiled again. He liked her smile.

"No, smarty pants. We're having a tossed salad, lasagna with fresh French bread and grated cheese. Is that okay with you, madam?" She sat about a foot away from him on the couch, but that was too far away, so he scooted closer.

"Oh my! That's just fine with me. But I told you about that salad stuff."

"I know, I know. But my mother fixed a salad every night; no matter what she cooked, she made a salad. So I'm pretty into salad. You don't have to eat it, you can just watch me." His finger traced the outline of her jaw.

Watching him was going to be a bigger problem than sitting next to him, she thought. "So do you want to talk now or after dinner?" she asked.

"That depends."

"On what?"

"On whether you're going to hear what I have to say and be open-minded to the idea, or if you're going to get on your soapbox and recite all the reasons I'm wrong." He watched as the worry shaded her eyes.

"Because I'm really hungry and I'd like to have a good meal with a beautiful woman sitting across from me."

"So are we talking now or not?" She looked confused.

Keith laughed at her confusion because in staring at her, he'd completely forgotten what they were talking about. "We can talk now if you want."

"I just want to get it over with," she shrugged. "And I promise I'll stay for dinner." She placed her hand on his knee. Keith took that small gesture as a good sign and pulled her even closer to him.

"Any closer, and I'll be in your lap."

"That sounds even better." Before she could protest, he scooped her up, placing her across his legs. "Comfy?" he asked.

"No, but I'm sure you are."

"I sure am, so don't even think about moving." He kissed her quickly, his lips brushing lightly against hers, a featherlike touch that rattled both of them. "Okay. So I've been thinking that maybe we have something going, and I'm really interested in pursuing that. What about you?" He decided to leave out the "L" word, for now. She didn't look like she was ready to accept that yet.

"What do I think about you pursuing whatever it is that you think we have going, or what do I think about what we have going?"

"Can I talk to the woman and not the counselor?" he asked.

"Okay. The *woman* is asking which question you'd like answered first?"

"I'd like to know how the woman feels about me."

"See, that's another question entirely." Cienna knew she was dodging all of his questions and wanted nothing more than to be able to confide her feelings in him. Still, she held back. There were no guarantees that this would work, and she wondered how she would cope when it was over. How would she continue to work with him after a failed relationship? She hadn't been able to do it before.

Mionne's words from earlier stuck in her mind. What if Keith was only looking to get her into his bed? What if this wasn't going to go any further than sex? Could she live with that? Could she accept that? More importantly, was there any truth to Mionne's accusations about her being afraid to take a chance?

"Cienna, in a minute you're going to piss me off."

"Whooooo, I'm scared of you." She tried to laugh away her nervousness. "Okay, okay. I have been feeling something between us. I'm not really sure if it's just sexual or something more. And as far as pursuing it, I haven't decided if that's possible or not. And as for how I feel about you, the jury's still out on that one, too." She said it all in one quick breath. "Next question."

Relieved that she hadn't shot him down completely, he shifted a little in the chair, pulling her even closer to him. He loved the feel of her in his arms. It was so natural, so comforting, so right. "Okay. That's a good start. Now, what is it that's not possible? You and I sleeping together or you and I having a serious relationship?"

"Both."

"Why?"

"Because if we sleep together, you may want more than sex. At least, I hope you want more than that. And a serious relationship is, as I said before, not on the agenda." She watched as his facial expression changed from optimism to defeat. "Don't get me wrong, I like you. I think I like you a little too much, but I'm just not sure I can handle a relationship right now, and I don't want to cheat you."

"Why don't we just follow our hearts, and you let me decide when I'm being cheated?" he asked. "Look, I understand where you're coming from about your career. Hell, a few weeks ago, I was in the same boat. But now things are different. I still want to be a judge, and I'm still gonna work my ass off to get there, but I want to be with you, too, and I'm gonna work just as hard to have that as well."

She sighed, "You see how you just said that? How you're so sure of that? I'm not. I can't sit here right now and tell you that I'm going to have both, because I don't know if I can."

She was afraid to tell him what she was really running from. She couldn't help acknowledging the feeling that Keith was different—that he saw something in her other than her looks, which amazed her. In fact, he seemed to not even notice how she looked. The bottom line was she was afraid of a repeat of the Bobby incident. She wanted so badly to explore the possibility of a relationship with Keith. But in the end, she admitted to him she wanted a partnership more.

"And you'd rather give up the personal for the professional?" He lifted one thick eyebrow in question.

"I'll have time for the personal later."

"My mother told me one time that you only have one true love, and the rest are just cheap substitutes. I hope you don't end up settling for substitutes, Cienna," he said finally.

She didn't know what to say in response to that. They were only supposed to be talking about starting a relationship. She hadn't even thought about true love and all that implied. He pulled her closer to him. And although she wanted to, she didn't pull away. Instead, she laced her fingers through his, enjoying the connection. He was steady, like a rock, she thought. Wistfully, she admitted to herself that was exactly what she needed.

The phone rang again, interrupting their solitude. Keith decided not to answer it out of fear that it would be Tyra again.

"Aren't you going to get that?" Cienna raised an eyebrow at him.

"Nope. Lasagna's ready," he announced, kissing her soundly on the lips and lifting her off his lap.

"It smells good." She tried to ignore the shrilling phone and followed him to the kitchen. Stainless steel gleamed from every corner as Keith opened the oven to pull out lasagna in an aluminum pan.

"I thought you said we weren't having a TV dinner?"

"This is not a TV dinner. It's an entrée. A family entrée, and it's great. I have it about three or four times a month. You'll love it." He carried the hot container into the dining room.

"I bet I will." Cienna followed him into the other room and took a seat at the long glass table. A nice floral arrangement would have been just lovely in the center, but this was a bachelor pad, so there was nothing adorning the table. The chairs were high-back pewter with thick gray cushions that matched the area rug covering the hardwood floor.

"I'll just dish your food up now since you don't eat salad," Keith told her as he cut into the hot noodles.

"Thank you." When there was a large slice of piping hot lasagna and a chunk of French bread sopping with butter in front of her, she bowed her head to say grace. Keith watched her as he had in the restaurant. She seemed serene when she prayed, as if she set everything else in the world aside for those few moments.

She finished and opened her eyes to find him staring at her. "What?" she asked, surprised to be under such close scrutiny.

"Oh, nothing. Sorry. I just like to watch you pray." Taking his seat, he lifted a bottle and poured dressing on his salad.

"Why? Don't you pray?" she asked curiously.

"No, not really. I mean, when I was little I used to go to church with my grandmother, but my mother never really got into it, so when I hit the teen years, I sort of let it go, too."

"That's a shame." Cienna shrugged her shoulders. "You should go back. It's hard enough trying to make it in this world, but without Jesus in your life, I don't know how people do it. I mean, I couldn't be without Him," she said seriously. "Maybe you can come with me one Sunday," she suggested, then thought maybe that was a mistake.

Keith, taking it as a good sign of the future, jumped at the invitation. "I'd love to." He saw her tense up and smiled to ease her worrying. The phone rang again. Keith looked into the living room and shook his head before resuming his meal.

"So, who are you ducking from?" Cienna asked before putting a small bite of lasagna into her mouth. He was right; it was good. As a matter of fact, it was almost as good as homemade.

"Nobody. Why do you think I'm ducking somebody?"

"Because you won't answer the phone when you obviously know who it is. It must be that woman that keeps calling the office," Cienna said lightly. She had wanted to ask him about that woman for a while now, but hadn't had the guts.

"How do you know about her? Never mind, I know...Reka." They both laughed. "I broke up with her a few weeks ago, but she's having a hard time accepting it."

"Really? Damn, you must be good."

"I don't know about that. I think it's more that she's a lunatic."

"Maybe you were the one who made her a lunatic."

"You sound like you want to find out what I did. Maybe experience it for yourself." He was daring her now.

"Maybe. But just so you know early on, I'm no lunatic. And I have no intention of becoming one, regardless of what skills you might possess." Cienna smiled and forked another chunk of lasagna into her mouth.

"Good, 'cause I'm sick of her. I'm about to catch a charge messin' around with her." Just then, the phone stopped as abruptly as it had begun. He wondered if Tyra had sensed his rage and decided to try back later.

CHAPTER FIFTEEN

After dinner, they moved back into the living room. This time, he didn't have to pull her close to him. She took a seat as close to him as she could get without landing on his lap again.

"So, I've been reading up on sexual harassment, and it's a lot bigger than I thought," Cienna began.

"Yeah, I've done a little research myself. In fact, I told Charles that I thought it was time we had something in place at the office. You know, something formal." Keith had his arm around her, and she rested her head on his shoulder.

"Maybe we should have a risk manager come in and evaluate what we really need. I mean, even though office disputes are fairly common, one thing that scares the hell out of risk managers and supervisors is the threat of a sexual harassment suit."

"And harassment allegations don't go away. After talking to you last night, I realized that we have a pretty sexually hostile work environment. And it's not just you. Kim Mation's been getting hit on by a lot of the associates, too," Keith told her. "Charles needs to address the situation now before somebody really gets pissed and files a suit."

"I never thought of filing a suit. I mean, I kind of just accepted it and went on. It didn't really bother me, because nobody touched me. I mean, they'd make comment—not vulgar or anything—just little comments about me being attractive and a particular outfit looking good on me. But they never touched me."

"Well, even the little comments need to stop. You've made it quite clear that you don't want to be involved with them in that way, and they need to respect that. And as for Simms, he needs his ass kicked. He's going to say the wrong thing to the wrong one, and one day they're gonna find his ass dead as a doornail." Keith tried to restrain the anger that bubbled inside him.

"You're probably right. Do you think I should press charges?"

"That's your call. Me, I would. Just to show that bastard that he can't get away with it. You know, there have to be more people in that office that he's harassed who've kept quiet. Keeping quiet affords him the opportunity to do it again."

"Obviously, he's threatening their jobs. Barber's report so much as says that." Cienna thought of the thinly veiled threat Simms had made to her earlier that day.

"That's true."

"I guess if I file suit, I should find an attorney, huh? You know any good plaintiff's attorneys?" She looked up at him and smiled.

"You know I do. Do you want me to call, or can you handle that?" He smoothed a loose strand of hair from her face.

"I can handle a phone call, but I'd like you to go with me when I meet with him." She watched the smile etch across his face and felt her insides melt. This man was dangerous, and she was falling so fast she could barely remember the arguments she had posed just a few hours ago.

"I'll be with you every step of the way."

"Thanks. I'm not going to do it right away though," she said.

"Don't mention it. Whenever you need me, I'll be there. That's what friends are for," he told her and meant it. He wanted to be her friend; he wanted to always be there for her, to provide her with whatever it was that she needed.

"I'm glad you're my friend." Searching his eyes for something, not really sure what, she watched him and waited.

"I'm glad I am, too."

Her eyes dropped to his lips and like a light bulb lighting up in her head, she realized what she was waiting for. She wanted him to touch her. She almost begged him to with her eyes. But his hands remained in his lap.

Deciding not to beat around the bush any longer she said, "I was wondering if my friend would like to kiss me, or is that crossing the line?" She watched him intently, waiting for his lips to touch hers.

For a moment, he was shocked speechless. Then her invitation registered clearly in his mind, and he whispered, "Friends usually don't do what I'm about to do." He leaned closer and took her mouth in a fierce motion.

Their tongues clashed, their arms entangled around each other, and all negative thoughts were vanquished from their minds. They were the only two people left in the world, and that suited them just fine.

When his hands couldn't satisfy themselves with touching her through her clothes, Keith pulled her shirt from the waist of her jeans and found the peak of her breast. Soft moans escaped Cienna's throat as her world continued to rock on the edge.

"Cienna, I need you," she heard Keith say in her ear. "I need you so bad." His tongue was in and out of her ear, inciting dampness between her legs; legs she now wrapped around him, bringing him closer to her.

"I don't know," she heard herself saying and cursed the words. She knew she wanted him. She knew he wasn't Bobby. The rest she could deal with later. But for sure she couldn't go home tonight and not know the touch of him, not know how it would feel to have him love her.

From a distance, she heard the snap on her jeans. Her eyes rolled back in her head as his hand slipped beneath the band of her panties with mild pressure. He cupped her mound, letting his fingers rest against the soft pad of hair while his tongue mingled desperately with hers. His fingers separated the pliant lips of her womanhood as he sought her puckered bud. Flicking the taut nub between his fingers, he swallowed her moans and pushed her further.

Tearing his lips from hers he begged, "Tell me you want me. Tell me you want this. I know you do. All you have to do is tell me." Keith was barely holding on. It was all he could do to touch her, to smell her and not take her completely. She had to make up her mind, and soon, or else they'd both be sorry.

"Please...," she murmured. "Please." The helpless cry escaped her lips.

He kissed her again, moving his tongue in her mouth to match the motion of his finger invading her secret place. Cienna bucked wildly beneath him.

"Say the words, Cienna. Say them! Say them!" he demanded. "Open your eyes and tell me what you want!"

Her eyes felt as if they were weighed down with lead as she struggled to open them. She licked her lips and stared into dark eyes intense with passion, passion that was all for her. She trusted him. She wanted him. She needed him.

"I want you. I want you inside me right now," she said finally. And Keith was undone.

In one minute flat, he had her in his bedroom on the king-sized bed. Her jeans lay on the floor, her shirt somewhere beside it. He stared at her lying there, clad only in her underwear. She wore simple cotton briefs with Victoria's Secret scribed across the band. No, they weren't silky, sexy thongs; they were simply underwear. Still, they drove him crazy.

He never remembered being this turned on before. When she held up her hands to him, he wanted to cry with joy. He'd waited a long time for this day. So he did something he hadn't done in years. He prayed that he'd be able to take things slow enough for them both to enjoy this first time.

On a ragged moan, he pulled her panties down her legs. Her arms tangled around his neck as she fought to bring him closer.

"Cienna." Her name escaped his lips just as he reached behind her to unclasp her bra.

When one of her hands snaked down the length of his chest past his stomach and gripped his penis, he tore at the bra, ripping it from her arms and tossing it across the room. His mouth, hot and wet, found her breasts, plump and tender, while her hand stroked him ardently.

With the last of his control withering quickly, Keith stood to rid himself of his clothes. Cienna studied him closely. He was wonderfully built; muscles bulged and stretched over his body, flexing in response to her uninhibited evaluation. His chest gleamed with a soft sheen of sweat, and his hips narrowed to the forest of dark hair that surrounded his rock hard penis. It jutted out in her direction, as if it were calling to her personally. She licked her lips in anticipation.

Keith stretched out on the bed and laid his hand on the flat of her stomach and let it rest there while he collected his thoughts. So many things he wanted to do to her, but he didn't know where to start.

"What's the matter?"

"Nothing. I'm just trying to think..." He watched the rise and fall of her breasts.

"Don't." She reached her hand up to cup his face. "Don't think." Rising up slightly on her elbows, she kissed him. Her tongue outlined his lips before claiming them completely. His hands moved to grip her hips, digging into the soft skin of her bottom.

He rested the tip of his penis at the door of her moist opening. Staying there a moment, he watched her react.

"Please, I need you now! Keith, please," she said, begging him to come to her. The sound was glorious to his ears. She *wanted* him, and she wanted him as badly as he wanted her.

He came into her gradually at first, savoring the feelings that washed over him slowly and painfully. Her walls swelled around his penis, trapping him inside her. Her juices puddled and dripped onto his swollen testicles.

Cienna held him firmly, closing her eyes to the darkness that had enveloped her.

"My God," he swore through clenched teeth.

"Keith." His name was all Cienna could manage. They were trapped, neither one able to move, neither one wanting to move.

When he started the timeless motion of love, Cienna lost all control, wrapped her legs around his waist and met him stroke-for-stroke as she climbed the mountain of ecstasy.

Keith pounded into her incessantly, giving her all he had, taking all she gave. The sloshing, slurping sound caused by her wetness and his desire enhanced his fervor, and he wished it would never end. He pulled out quickly, giving himself a reprieve, as he wasn't ready for the sweetness to end.

"Don't leave me," she whispered.

"I'm not leaving you, baby. I've got something else for you." He reached into his nightstand and retrieved a glossy black vibrator. He watched as her eyes widened with shock. "Just relax. Trust me." Licking his lips, he clicked the mechanism on.

The slow humming approached her cove. He gently moved it over her clit, studying her face for her reaction. Her eyes closed and her legs opened wider.

Keith's eyes were drawn to the sight before him. She was gorgeous all over. The lips of her vulva parted and he watched as her nectar glistened and seeped from her. Using his fingers to further part her lips he drove his toy up and down, watching her wriggle beneath him.

Every now and then, he would dip his finger inside her, returning it quickly to his mouth, tasting her sweetness. "Yeah, baby. Look at you; you are so beautiful. I love looking at you. Touching you. This is driving me crazy," he said before he placed his toy inside her.

"Oh…oh…damn, that feels good." Cienna wriggled and grasped the sheets. She floated somewhere in the room, feeling light and complete. She heard her juices swishing against the smooth plastic of his toy as he moved it in and out of her faster and faster.

"You want more?" he asked as he watched her mouth moving silently. "Tell me what you want, baby,"

Instead of telling him, she closed her legs and rose up to kneel before him, his toy sliding completely out of her. Her breasts were in his face, and he tossed the toy aside to take them into his mouth. Cienna cradled his head before she straddled him.

His legs were off the side of the bed, and his feet were firmly planted on the stone gray carpet when Cienna grabbed his shaft and came down over him slowly.

"Damn!" was all he managed to say before she started riding him hard. Her breasts bounced up and down, and he sat up so that they were in his face slapping against his cheeks. Guttural groans rumbled deep in his chest before he opened his mouth, growling like a wounded animal.

"Is this what *you* wanted?" she asked him.

"Yes, baby. Yes!" he said to her. He gripped her butt as she continued to move. The room began to swim as he felt her pouring out onto him again. He reveled in the pleasure she was getting. "Oh baby!!" he roared.

"You ready to cum, baby?" Cienna asked him.

"Oh, God, make me cum, make Daddy cum!" He was yelling louder now.

Cienna pushed him back on the bed to get more leverage over him. She pumped mercilessly, stopping briefly to pursue a circular motion. Keith lay on the bed with his eyes closed and his mouth wide open. His hands gripped her hips and gently lifted her up before pulling her forcibly back down. "Aaargh! Yeah, this is so good. You are so good!" he was saying.

"Oh, baby, I'm gonna cum again!" Cienna screamed.

Keith placed his fingers between her legs to take the hot liquid into his hands. "Ahhhh, yeah! Yeah! Let it all out, baby, let it all out."

Cienna's climax brought out new energy in her. She quickly turned the other way, still straddling him, but with her back to his face now. She placed his large shiny manhood inside her and rode it for the final mile.

Keith roared in completion and held Cienna's hips tightly in place as he spilled himself deep within her womb.

"No one but you. Only you, Cienna. Only you," he repeated over and over again as he lost it all.

He unconsciously gave her what no man had ever given her before. Cienna thought she would cry with joy and had to concentrate hard to keep that from happening. He was deep inside her now, and she felt the slight pulsing of his release. She held tightly to his thighs for fear of tipping over onto the floor. When he was completely drained, he lifted her up and cradled her in his arms. He loved this woman. The feeling encompassed him completely. But he didn't want to scare her, so he kept the thoughts in his mind.

"Am I hurting you?" he said as he loosened his grip on her.

"No, I'm fine," she said quickly.

"Cienna?" He called her name from where his head rested in the crook of her neck.

"Yes?" she answered, not knowing what to expect.

"No regrets?" he asked.

She smiled and kissed his shoulder again. "No regrets."

CHAPTER SIXTEEN

Cienna walked with a much lighter step this morning. Stepping off the elevator, she greeted Reka without stopping to chat and went straight into her office.

Her message light was flashing, and she groaned at the thought of answering it. When she arrived home last night, well, earlier this morning, she had three hang-ups on her answering machine. She had a sinking feeling that these messages might be more of the same.

Dropping her briefcase under the desk, she sat in her chair and booted up her computer. She decided to go through her emails first, then tackle the voice-mail. As her fingers ran lightly across the keys, she thought about Keith and the things they'd done to each other last night. Her body tingled, and she shivered as the memories aroused her. Deep into her thoughts, she didn't hear anyone approach until papers were slid onto her desk in front of her. She looked up just in time to see Mionne's back.

"Charles wants those reviewed and signed by lunch time," she told Cienna as she walked out of the office.

"Okay." Mionne was out the door before the word was out of Cienna's mouth. Shaking her head, Cienna wondered what was going on with her friend or the woman she'd thought was her friend.

After careful evaluation, Cienna had come to the conclusion that she'd done nothing wrong where Mionne was concerned. She had only tried to be a friend. This sudden animosity Mionne showed towards her was neither warranted nor excusable. After all, it wasn't her fault Lee had been a cheater.

The elevator stopped, and Keith stepped off. Dressed in a black double-breasted suit, crisp white dress shirt and black silk tie, he knew he looked good, and he felt even better. He'd finally gotten a taste of Cienna, and instead of being content, his hunger had only increased. Her lips had been beyond soft, her moans surpassing the sweetest love song; her release had shaken him to the core, pulling him deeper into the ocean of love.

He'd awakened this morning eager to see her, itching to hold her. He'd begged her to stay, but she'd gone home anyway. Afraid to push, he'd reluctantly let her go. Waking up in that bed where she had lain, in that room where her voice had echoed words of desire, of fulfillment, of pleasure, he'd missed her instantly.

But right now, he had something important to take care of. Something he needed to nip in the bud, for his own peace of mind.

"Mr. Simms has a meeting in about ten minutes, but I'm sure he won't mind seeing you," the gold-toothed diva told him. "I know I sure don't," she murmured when Keith walked past her desk towards Simms' office.

Keith ignored her and focused on the matter at hand. He didn't bother to knock, just opened the door and stepped in. Simms was on the phone, but raised his brow in question as Keith came in and took a seat. Keith waited patiently until the conversation was finished and Simms had hung up the phone.

"Did we have an appointment, Mr...," he paused, as if trying to remember Keith's name.

But Keith wasn't fooled; he'd seen the recognition in the man's eyes the moment he stepped into the room. "This isn't a business visit, so we can cut the formalities." Keith sat with his legs spread wide, his elbows resting on his knees, his eyes trained on Simms.

"I understand you got a little carried away with Ms. Turner the other day."

Simms' eyes bulged as he prepared to deny Keith's allegations.

Keith continued. "I'm going to say this one time and one time only. Keep your sexual overtures to yourself. She's not interested, and I'm not the cops so I won't arrest you, but I don't have any qualms about beating the hell out of you should you step out of line again." His voice was even, his eyes dangerous.

"I'm sure I have no idea what you're talking about. Maybe Ms. Turner was mistaken." Simms shrugged.

"And maybe brown cows piss chocolate milk. Don't insult my colleague or me. I know what you did, and I know you've done it before. But now you've messed with the wrong one."

"Is that a threat?" Simms looked toward his phone, wondering how quickly he could have security summoned to his office.

Keith stood and calmly buttoned his suit jacket, "No, sir, that's a bona fide promise. Step out of line with her again, and I'll break your neck!" With a curt nod in Simms' direction, Keith walked out of his office.

Simms sat back in his chair reviewing the events that had just taken place. Reaching for the phone, he dialed a number he knew all too well.

"Hello?" a male voice answered.

"Hey, we've got a problem," he told the man on the other end.

The afternoon had dragged on with Reka constantly interrupting and Mionne giving her cold responses. Cienna had a headache. Her motion to compel was due by four-thirty and she was hungry. She had skipped lunch in an effort to have the motion ready on time, and now she was paying the price. Her blood sugar was low, her temper was short…and she missed Keith.

He'd called her to say a quick good morning, but then he'd been in and out of the office for the remainder of the day. It was silly, she knew, but she really wanted to see him. She wanted to hear his voice, see his face. With a start, she realized that his mere presence in her life had changed her. He'd made her think a real relationship was possible again. That maybe, just maybe, this time around things would be different.

Rubbing her tired eyes, she sighed, "He's only a man, Cee, get a grip." She laughed to herself. "I must be crazy sitting here talking to myself."

"No, crazy is when you answer yourself." Keith appeared at her door as if her thoughts alone had summoned him.

She looked up to see the man who'd made her weak with pleasure last night, the man who'd inched his way into her heart, and she smiled. "Then I'm halfway there."

Keith had been happy to see her and even happier to see the way her face lit up when she saw him. He had thought about her all day. Her smile, her scent, her touch. He had missed her terribly and couldn't wait until he'd cleared most of the relevant stuff from his desk so he could come and spend some time with her. Closing the door behind him, he thought to himself, you've got it pretty bad.

Cienna watched him take a seat, admiring the way his muscles bulged against the material of his dress shirt, remembering the feel of the hard mass of his chest beneath her hands. Her fingers tingled with the urge to touch him again. He sat back in the chair and lifted a hand to drag down his face, drawing her attention to his strong jaw, his full lips, his chocolate brown eyes. She almost moaned. Damn, he looked good!

"So what's up? Having a rough day?" he asked.

"Can you tell?" Motioning towards the unfinished pleading on her desk, she sighed, "Deadline."

"On?"

"On how bad I want to win this case."

"So how's it going?"

"About another hour, and it should be ready to fly. How was your meeting?" She gave up trying to work on the paper for the moment.

"Long and not prosperous. They won't settle, we're gonna have to go to trial." He removed his jacket, throwing it on the other chair.

Cienna tried not to look interested, but, oh, was it hard. "So what are your chances at trial?"

"Dismal at best." He wondered if she had any idea how sexy she was. How the folds of her dress fell perfectly over her breasts, camouflaging the round softness he knew hid beneath.

"Looks like we're both batting a thousand today," she said, ironically. She hunched her shoulders. Her vagina pulsed with arousal, and she shifted in the chair. Propping her arms up on the desk, she picked up a pencil and twisted it between her fingers as a distraction.

"Yeah, well, that can be remedied." Keith gave her a lopsided grin. He sat back further in the chair, his legs wide apart, his arms resting on the sides.

"Suggestions?" Cienna arched an eyebrow.

Damn, that was sexy! Office relationships definitely had their perks, he thought. "Dinner at seven."

"Just dinner?" she queried.

"And dessert, of course." The corners of his mouth lifted into a smug grin.

Cienna shook her head. "Dinner will be just fine. I'll skip dessert." Dropping the pencil she sat back in her chair. The pencil hadn't distracted her one bit. "It's addictive."

"You better believe it is." He licked his lips and smiled.

CHAPTER SEVENTEEN

"Maybe we should shut it down for a while. Just until you get this deal with the state done. There's too much attention on you right now."

"I know. Have you heard anything from her?" Simms asked the man sitting across from him.

"No, but she made a point of telling me what went down between you two." The man shook his head. "I told you to leave her alone. I told you she was crazy and she wasn't worth it."

"Oh, she was worth it," Simms sighed. "Believe me, she was worth it. But I've moved on now. Bigger and better things have come up."

"Oh yeah? You need to leave that one alone, too. She's not game, I can promise you that," the man warned.

"She just thinks she's not game. She needs a little convincing."

"Don't take his threats lightly, man. I think he's hung up on her, and you know how a man can get about his territory. Just let her be."

"She's in my blood."

"Forget it. You're going to get us caught. I tried to warn you before. I've got a lot at stake here, and I don't want to go down just because some woman's got you sprung. Now leave her alone, let her do her job. She'll get these cases settled, and you'll get that contract. Then we can move on. Business has been good. In another three years, we'll both be able to retire. St. Martin is looking mighty good to me right about now." Simms' friend stood and walked around the office.

"You taking the missus with you?"

"Yeah, man, it's cheaper to keep her."

Both men laughed.

"I figured the same. Natalie's been cool. She's stood by me. I guess I should start thinking about settling with her and focusing on our future. But man, we've had a good thing going for a while now."

"Yeah, but all good things must come to an end. It's just too dangerous, and, besides, we're getting too old for this stuff. It was a good idea back in college when it was all about sex, but now we're older…"

"And it's still all about sex." Simms finished his friend's sentence.

The men laughed and talked about the financial status of their thriving partnership, then went their separate ways. It was time to dissolve the business that had made both of them what they were today. But it was okay. They'd done well for the last twenty years, and now they were going to go out with a bang. Cienna Turner was going to see to that.

"Simms has called me four times since Tuesday," Cienna said to Keith when they were alone in her office Friday morning. "He's sent me flowers and two cards in apology."

"Damn, how big a fool is he? Doesn't he know that he's incriminating himself?" Keith said.

"Whose side are you on?" Cienna asked mildly.

"Sorry, always the defense attorney. Anyway, I've been in contact with Barber's attorney, and he's asking for $1.5 million. I told him he was dreaming, to call me back in three days with something a little more reasonable. I figure we'd be good if we could get all three settled under a million-dollar cap."

"Do you think they'll go for it?"

"I'm almost positive. I talked to Charles this morning, and he thought a quick settlement was the best option. Actually, he wants it wrapped up as quickly as possible. He said close it today if we could."

"Today? That's a little unreasonable, isn't it? I mean, it's only actually our first real meeting with Simms. We haven't deposed anyone, and we haven't talked to that many witnesses." Cienna seemed confused.

"That's what I thought when he called me into his office this morning. But he said he knew we had a meeting with Simms today and he wanted this case resolved as soon as possible. My guess is the governor's about to award that big contract, and they want Simms' plate clear to accept it."

"Still, how does he think we're supposed to convince all the parties involved to take a settlement in one day? It just doesn't make sense."

"No, it doesn't. But I'd like to do just that. I don't want you to have to deal with Simms any more than is absolutely necessary. If we can wrap this up quickly; it's over, it's done. We can move on, and he can move on." Keith moved from the spot he had been standing in across the room from her. He hadn't touched her since reluctantly leaving her apartment last night. He needed to touch her. Needed to be near her.

"So he can move on to the next victim," Cienna replied.

Keith was behind her desk now, grabbing the back of her chair, turning it so that she faced him. "You can still press charges against him or file a complaint yourself."

"I know," she sighed. She was a little disappointed. If they settled the case today or within the next week, it wouldn't be enough. There were no revealing depositions or new witnesses to blow open the plaintiff's case. It would just be money in exchange for Simms' guilt. Somehow, she wasn't really satisfied with that.

Keith stooped down in front of her, taking her hands in his. They fit perfectly, and he stared down at her lighter complexion against his own darker skin. Her hands were soft, her fingers narrow. He remembered the feel of them around his manhood and felt the familiar surge of lust going through him. Tearing his eyes away from her hands, he focused on her face; the pretty face that had evaded him for so long and now occupied his every thought. He loved this woman. Beyond anything else in this world, he loved her and wanted nothing else but to protect her.

"What else is bothering you?" he asked.

Cienna watched him carefully. She'd felt the warmth of his hands as he held hers tightly. She'd seen something in his eyes. Something different than she'd seen before. He was changing. Things between them were changing. And she was afraid. She didn't quite know how to deal with all these changes in her life at one time. She pulled her hands from his hold. "Nothing. We should get ready for our meeting." She shifted in her chair and began to shuffle papers around.

Keith was disheartened. He'd opened himself to her, offered her his help and she'd shut down. She'd looked at him and turned away. What was it going to take for her to trust him? To trust their relationship?

He didn't know. He simply didn't know. But he was going to find out. Maybe not right now. No, now was not the time, but she would tell him. He would find out what it was that continued to hold her back from him. "You're right," he said.

He stood and returned to the other side of her desk, grabbing his briefcase from the chair. "So we'll go see Simms and propose the settlement." He spoke decisively, as if he were focused on the task at hand, but didn't chance looking at her again, for he knew he'd grab her. He'd probably shake her until she told him what had happened to her in the past that made her resist him the way she was. He knew that wouldn't go well for either of them, so instead, he moved toward the door and waited for her to follow.

Cienna grabbed her briefcase. "We'll propose the settlement, and then we'll talk to Charles."

Keith turned at her last statement. "Talk to Charles?"

"If we're wrapping this case up so nicely and neatly, it'll get Simms off without so much as a slap on the wrist. He'll do it again and again, as long as he can get away with it. If I file a complaint, I won't settle. I'd like Charles to know that up front." She was serious; her mind was made up. If she had to let him slide through on this case, she would. But she'd damn sure hang him on her own. She'd saved every card, every message. And his carefully veiled threat still loomed in her mind. She would take him down a notch or two if it were the last thing she did.

Keith stared at her. Her eyes were fixed, her face serious. She was determined, and he was glad. He'd wanted to go to Charles from the start. Yes, he was glad she was going to tell him. "Good. Then let's get this show on the road." He opened the door and stood beside it, waiting for her to pass through.

Simms was in his office waiting—waiting for the chance to see her again. He knew that Page would probably be with her, but that was okay, as long as he got a chance to see her. He hadn't wanted a woman so badly in years.

A knock at his door signaled their arrival, and he smoothed down his tie and sat straight up in his chair before telling them to come in.

"Good afternoon," he spoke jovially.

"Mr. Simms." Keith nodded his head curtly.

Cienna remained quiet. She wasn't sure if she'd be able to sit here and proceed as if nothing had happened between them since the last time she'd been in this office. But she was going to try.

Keith motioned toward a chair for her and took her briefcase so she could sit down. Placing her brief-case on the floor, he took the seat next to hers.

"Mr. Simms, we'd like to discuss the possibility of a settlement." Keith began by removing a notepad from his briefcase.

"We believe this is best for all involved parties," Cienna chimed in. "After a careful review of the reports and all the facts, we believe that this case will be best ended by a monetary settlement offer to the plaintiffs."

"I didn't do anything untoward to those people." Simms spoke clearly.

"You had sex with your administrative assistant," Keith said incredulously. He couldn't believe the man continued to think that the things he did were justified.

"It wasn't rape. She agreed," he defended himself.

Keith continued his interrogation. "Did she agree on her own, or was she intimidated into agreeing? Did you not tell her she would be fired if she didn't submit?" He had hoped they wouldn't have to get into all this with an impending settlement, but obviously Simms needed to see the error of his ways.

"I wouldn't have fired her. She just needed a little push. You know, sometimes women need a little push." His eyes roamed toward Cienna. "They can't quite make up their own minds sometimes."

Cienna shifted in her chair uncomfortably. "A little push constitutes assault. Job intimidation constitutes sexual harassment. What part of that don't you understand?"

When Simms didn't answer, Keith continued, "What about Barber? Do men need a little push, too?"

"He was stupid. Always bragging about how many boyfriends he had and how good he was in bed. I just wanted to give him a taste of a real man. You know, to shut him up a bit."

"So a real man has sex with an IT technician in his office and then promises to give him a promotion?"

"I never promised him anything," Simms replied.

Tired of the discussion, Keith flipped through the pages of his notepad quickly. "We want to offer them each one million."

"A million bucks? That's insane. They wanted it, too!" Simms argued. "The women flaunted themselves in front of me in those tiny little skirts and low-cut blouses, and when I touched them they just giggled. Oh, yeah, they wanted it and they enjoyed it! They enjoyed every minute of it! Just like you would." He leered at Cienna.

Cienna stared at him in shock. Had he just said that to her? Had he just said that in front of Keith? Out of the corner of her eye, she could see Keith's hand fisting at his side.

"Mr. Simms! That is enough! We're telling you as your attorneys how we think it's best to handle this case. Now, if you disagree, then maybe you should find other counsel."

Simms still stared at Cienna, his eyes glazed and dilated. "You sat in that club with that tight little dress on and tried to play hard-to-get. Then Charles sent you to me. I was so happy when I saw you. I couldn't thank ol' Charlie enough." Simms licked his lips and stood.

Cienna saw Keith drop his notepad and reached out to grab hold of his arm. She steadied him with a look. "Mr. Simms, we are going to go now and ask that you contact Charles with regard to your opinions of the settlement we've proposed." Cienna stood and picked up her briefcase.

Simms was around the desk in a second, reaching for her. "No, honey," he started. "We…"

Whatever else he intended to say or do went unsaid and undone, cancelled by Keith. In a fury, he barreled a fist directly into Simms' leering face.

Cienna heard the distinctive sound of flesh hitting flesh and watched as Simms fell backwards to the floor. Blood quickly spurted from his nose and ran down his face, staining the front of his shirt. Keith grabbed Cienna's hand and dragged her to the door.

"I'm gonna have you arrested for this," Simms called from where he still sat on the floor.

"I warned you, Simms," Keith said. He stood at the door barely restraining his fury, wanting nothing more than to go back and pound into his face some more. But Cienna pulled on his arm and they left.

In the car, they were silent. Cienna didn't know what to say, and Keith didn't want to say the wrong thing. He saw that she was shaking, but he didn't know if he was the one who had upset her or if it was Simms. All he knew was that he'd probably never make judge now. Amazingly, that didn't matter now. Charles would probably fire him for hitting a client. He didn't care. None of that mattered. All that mattered to him was the look he'd seen in Simms' eyes—the look of a sick, evil man intent on having his way with Cienna. He'd wanted to reach over the desk and hit him from the moment he looked her way. But he had refrained for Cienna's sake. But when Simms reached to touch her...He couldn't have stopped himself even if he had wanted to. He could have killed him. Had Cienna not been there to stop him, he didn't know what he might have done.

Cienna's insides shook with shock. She wanted to say something, anything, but she remained quiet. What would happen now? She wouldn't make partner, that was for sure. And Keith, well, he probably wouldn't make judge either. Maybe this was all her fault. For a brief moment, she allowed herself that idea. Then she tossed it aside. Simms was sick; it was as simple as that. She'd read about these kinds of people before. Obsessed with sex, obsessed with the dominance and superiority it gave them. That had nothing to do with her, and she wouldn't allow herself any blame in what had taken place.

Before she knew it, they had pulled into the office garage. Keith put the car in park and turned off the ignition. He rested his head against the headrest and closed his eyes. "We're going to go in and tell Charles everything that's happened, from the beginning. Then we're going to tell him what we recommend. Settlement, quick and simple." He didn't turn in her direction. He didn't open his eyes. His jaw was tight, his hands fisted at his sides.

"Fine." Her answer was curt and, to her own ears, sounded blasé and inconsequential.

"Cienna, what did you want me to do? Did you want him to touch you? Because that's what he was about to do? I couldn't sit there and watch it happen. Something changed with him right before our eyes, and it scared me to think of what he might do to you." Keith had turned to face her, finally, his dark eyes searching hers for forgiveness, for reconciliation.

She couldn't believe it. Did he really think she was angry with him? That she would be anything but supremely grateful for what he'd done to protect her? "I'm not angry with you, if that's what you think." She blinked in confusion.

"You're not?"

"No! If I'm angry with anybody, it's Charles. Simms is his friend, which means he probably has some clue as to how sick this man really is. Yet he wanted us to go in and defend this case, make it all better for Simms." She sighed deeply. "You're right. We're going to go into that office and tell Charles what a slime his friend is and what he tried to pull with me. Then we're going to settle this damned case and move on."

Her voice had gotten stronger, louder, more confident as she continued to speak. Keith watched her lips moving, enjoying the sound of her voice. A small vein pumped quickly in her neck, and he smiled. She was sexy when she got angry. He reached over and cupped her chin, turning her to face him. "You are so beautiful," he told her.

"That's not exactly what I want to hear right now," Cienna sighed. She didn't want to hear it. She'd heard it enough in her lifetime. But coming from Keith it was different. It sounded different. It sounded sincere. Like an endearment instead of a proclamation. She turned her face into his hand, enjoying the feel of his skin against hers.

When she looked at him, he almost told her. He almost admitted that he loved her. Then he looked deeper into her eyes and saw the fear. The fear that he had yet to chase away. His heart ached for that part of her he still could not reach.

"We should probably go," she suggested. She didn't want to put this off any longer than she had to.

"You're right," he agreed. He got out of the car and walked around to open the door for Cienna. When she stepped out, he closed the door, grabbed her by the arms and pulled her close to him. His lips found hers in a desperate search for her feelings. He wanted to know if she wanted him. If she wanted to be with him as much as he wanted to be with her.

She melted in his arms, giving him all that she had, all that she could give at the moment. He took it willingly, understanding that there was more she held back but accepting her offering just the same.

"Remember, we're in this together," he whispered against her still parted lips. "No regrets."

"No regrets," she sighed.

CHAPTER EIGHTEEN

"You are going to regret this, Charles Benton. You mark my words, you will live to regret this!" Mionne's voice echoed throughout the office floor.

Cienna and Keith had just stepped off the elevator and were headed towards Charles' office when they heard Mionne's voice. She had come out of Charles' office fussing and issuing threats. Cienna and Keith had stopped short to watch the scene before them.

"I've been sorry for quite some time now! You've worn out your welcome." Charles stood in the doorway of his office yelling right back at Mionne.

Cienna thought she had walked into some prime-time drama for a moment. It didn't seem as if she was in an office, a place of business. Obviously, there was a lot going on here that neither she nor Keith knew about. Charles and Mionne's words almost seemed too personal to be work related.

Keith cleared his throat loudly. Charles spotted them first and motioned for them to come into his office. Mionne looked up as she approached them and rolled her eyes.

Cienna stepped in front of her. "Mionne, what's going on?"

Mionne looked at her and laughed, an ugly, chilling sound escaping her throat. "Your ship's about to sink, too," she told her and laughed even louder.

Keith took Cienna's hand and led her into Charles' office and closed the door. Whatever that little scene was about, they were better off not knowing, he thought. At least not until they finished their own business with Charles.

"I've been waiting for you two," Charles spoke tersely. Taking a seat in his chair, he waited until they were both seated before proceeding. "I got a call from Simms."

"Charles, before you even begin, we have something to tell you." Keith looked at Cienna. Cienna nodded her head, assuring him that she was ready to go through with it.

Cienna cleared her throat and sat up straight in her chair. "I met Simms about a month ago in a club in Manhattan. He hit on me, and I left. When you assigned me to this case, I didn't recognize Simms as being the same man from the club. When I met with him alone, he made it perfectly clear who he was and proceeded to make unwanted advances towards me. I warned him several times that his advances were neither welcome nor shared, but he continued. It was my intention to see this case through before doing anything with regard to the harassment, but now things have changed."

"He made another play for her today. Right in front of me, the idiot tried to attack her!" Keith's voice boomed.

"As I understand it, Keith, you threatened him yesterday." Charles shot Keith a heated glare.

Cienna stared at Keith as well. She didn't know that Keith had seen Simms on his own.

"You're damned right I did! I told him if he made another advance toward her, I was going to break his neck, and I meant it!"

"So you broke his nose instead?" Charles frowned.

Keith defended his actions. "I said he made a move for her."

"I wasn't aware of that. I'll take care of it. But you are off the case. Simms has threatened to press charges if you come near him again," Charles told Keith pointedly. "And he wants you to continue with the case." He looked towards Cienna.

Cienna gasped, clutching the arms of the chair. "No!" she all but yelled. "I can't. I won't!" Keith reached for her but drew back as her eyes found his, giving him silent warning.

"What? What do you mean you can't? Just a couple of weeks ago, you were telling me that you didn't need to work with anybody. Now you want to back down?" Charles seemed shocked.

Cienna struggled for the right words to say. Keith took her hand in his, looking straight at Charles. "Haven't you heard anything she said? She is not working with him. I'll finish the case. We need to settle this, Charles. Simms is guilty, and there is no way we can get around it. I don't have to go near him to settle each case for a million dollars." Keith tried to speak reasonably but rage soared through him like boiling lava about to erupt.

"Cienna, I know it'll be hard, but…," Charles continued.

"But nothing. I won't do it." Partnership or not, she wasn't going to work with that man again. She didn't want to settle his case; she didn't want to see his face again. All she wanted to do right now at this very moment was get the hell out of this office as quickly as possible. Charles hadn't said a word about Simms' advances towards her. He had neither defended her nor cursed Simms for his stupidity. No, he had sat in his big mahogany chair dishing out orders as if she were some insignificant peon under his control.

"Okay, we'll work out a settlement, but he wants her," Charles said in a strained voice.

"I'm sorry, I don't mean it the way it sounded."

"I'll handle the case from here, or you can do it yourself. I don't want Cienna dealing with him again." Keith was trying his best not to sound like a furious boyfriend, even though that was what he was. He tried to recover. "I mean, it's not necessary to put her through that." He knew Cienna still didn't want their relationship to become public knowledge throughout the office.

"Are you going to press charges, Cienna?" Charles asked.

Afraid that Charles was not entirely on her side, she responded, "I haven't made a final decision yet. I do know that I won't work with him again. I can't defend him when I know for a fact that he's guilty."

"Guilty until proven innocent. Isn't that what we do?" Charles asked.

"No, that's what *you* do because he didn't say those things to *you*. He didn't look at you the way he looked at me." Shaking her head, she struggled not to break down. "He didn't make you feel cheap and disrespected."

"I understand that it was horrible, and I'm not excusing him. I just need to make the best professional decision, despite how outraged I am personally," Charles answered.

"I've made the best overall decision for me, and if that affects my career, then so be it." Cienna stood to leave. She hadn't gone in there with the intent to quit, but Charles didn't seem to understand the severity of the situation.

Walking back to her office she wondered what had just happened. Had she quit? Or was she fired? She wasn't quite sure.

"Is she okay?" Charles asked Keith after Cienna walked out, leaving the two men to stare after her.

"No, but I think she will be. This was hard for her, Charles. Simms has some serious problems."

"Yeah, I kind of thought so. But I never thought he'd be stupid enough to bother her. I've known him for a long time, so I know a little about his escapades. I think he may have gone too far this time," Charles commented.

"I think so, too. At any rate, I'll get started on the settlement negotiations." Keith was about to walk out of Charles' office when an alarming statement stopped him.

"But she is hot, isn't she? I mean, can you blame a man for trying?" Charles wore a sickly grin on his face.

Keith pondered his response, his career flashing before him, along with thoughts of punching Charles squarely in his jaw. "You know, Charles, I think it may be time to put a sexual harassment policy in place around here," Keith said to his boss and former mentor.

Cienna was seething with anger. Charles hadn't offered her one ounce of support. In fact, he'd all but dismissed her allegations against his friend. She paced her office, wondering what her next step should be. Should she leave? Just get up and go? No, she should call that lawyer and tell him she was ready to hang Simms by his toenails and to hell with the deal he had going with the state and the business it would bring the firm.

She really didn't know what to do. All she knew was that none of this would have ever happened had it not been for Raleigh Simms.

Keith went to her office as soon as he finished talking with Charles and was dismayed to find her gone. A call to the front desk told him that she had left for the day. Dammit! Why hadn't she waited for him? Hadn't she agreed that they were in this together? And now she was gone. He had to find her; she was in no shape to be alone. And he realized he didn't want her to be alone. Not ever again did he want her to be alone. He wanted to be there. He wanted to be her shoulder to cry on, the person she could lean on. He wanted to be everything to her, the way she had come to be everything to him.

There weren't many people left in the office now. Since it was after six on a Friday, most had left for the weekend. After seeing his car in the garage, she had taken the service elevator so she wouldn't be seen. The gold-toothed hussy was gone for the day, her computer and radio turned off. Her footsteps were muffled as she walked across the familiar gray carpet towards his office.

She knew exactly what she was about to do, knew that it was necessary for her as well as all those other unsuspecting women he'd had doing his bidding. Her purse bounced against her left side as she walked slowly down the hall, the heavy metal inside banging against her hip.

When she reached his open doorway, she watched him work for a moment. He looked so normal, so at-ease. Except for the bandage on his nose. She unzipped her purse, grasped the cool gun inside, pulled it out and pointed it at him.

Simms heard the click of the safety being released and looked up to see her standing there. "What the hell do you think you're doing?"

She walked toward him slowly, taking her time. She wanted him to see her. To see what he had done to her. She was tired of men; tired of the games they played with women. She had had enough. And now both of them were going to pay.

"This is ridiculous! What do you think you're going to do with that?" Simms stood, pushing his chair backwards so hard it slammed against the credenza.

"I'm doing what a lot of women wish they had the guts to do," she told him. She stopped directly in front of his desk. She wanted it to be at close range, so there would be no mistake about her intentions. She wanted him dead. Him and Charles, she wanted them both dead. They had used her and underestimated her intelligence. Well, she was going to have the last laugh.

"We can work this out. Just sit down, and we can talk," Simms stalled. "Or do you want to go and get some dinner? I haven't eaten yet."

She laughed. Her chest rumbled with the irony of his question. *Now* he wanted to take her out? "Oh no, sweetie, you don't need to worry about dinner. You see, where you're about to go, an empty stomach is the least of your worries. The undertakers will appreciate it." There was so much she thought she wanted to say—words she wanted him to hear before he died. But at this moment, she was more concerned with getting it over with. He was a sorry excuse for a man, and she was going to put an end to his miserable life.

"Don't do this. You'll go to jail. You might even get the death penalty," Simms warned.

"Then, I'll see you in hell," she said just before pulling the trigger.

CHAPTER NINETEEN

Cienna paced her apartment, not really sure how she felt about what had just happened. Not only had Simms tried to put the moves on her with Keith present, but Charles had brushed off the fact that his friend was guilty. He had been too concerned about wrapping the case up and catering to his friend's every demand to acknowledge that Cienna had been violated.

She had been embarrassed and outraged. And all of this had taken place in front of Keith, who had truly disappointed her. She'd wanted him to tell Charles he had to represent his friend himself. She'd wanted him to stalk out of Charles' office with her, to leave Charles standing there looking foolish. But he hadn't done any of that. Instead, Keith had offered to handle the case himself. For all his talk, it seemed that his ambitions were more important to him than she was.

In the end, he would settle the case. He would get all the glory. He would become a judge, and she would be…Where? Where would she be? She didn't know if she still had a job. And right about now, she didn't really care.

She paced the floor of her apartment wondering what she should do next. She needed someone to talk to. But who? Mionne was angry with her. Her mother wouldn't understand. And Keith—Keith was taking care of his business.

Cienna had spent the last few weeks dreading someone at work finding out about her and Keith, hoping that it wouldn't stifle her career if they did. She'd spent endless nights praying that he wouldn't hurt her the way Bobby had. And finally, she'd come to believe that he was different. That he wasn't Bobby.

And to his credit, he was different. He knew how to treat a woman. He knew how to touch a woman, how to make a woman fall in love with him. But now, it seemed she was insignificant in his scheme of things. She should have remembered that day in the lunchroom when he'd told her that he didn't have time for a family because he'd always wanted to become a judge. Apparently, his ambition was more important to him than she was.

She stuffed her fist into her mouth to stifle her cry. She'd been a fool. She should have listened to Mionne. Keith had wanted her only for sex. And she had willingly given him that. Along with the Simms case to add to his résumé.

Unable to stand the flurry of emotions soaring through her, Cienna went into her bedroom. Reaching into the back of her closet, she pulled out an old black duffle bag. Quickly and without really thinking, she began to stuff clothes into the bag. What she was doing, she really didn't know. Where she was going, she really didn't care. The point was she had to get away. There was too much going on here, at work, in her life, in her apartment...in Keith's apartment.

She shook her head at those memories and the stirrings that began deep inside her as she thought about the nights they had spent together. Those memories weren't going to help her now. She had to figure out what her next move was going to be. Maybe she would just go to another firm. Start all over. Again. The thought sat in her stomach like a rock, and she closed her eyes to dismiss it.

Satisfied that she had all she needed in her bag, she snatched up her purse and made her way to the door. She wondered briefly if she should call Keith. Should she leave him a note? Would he even care that she was gone?

Suddenly, her heart began to hammer in her chest, and and her palms began to sweat. A panic attack. Just like before. Just like the days she'd had to go to work and face the ridicule of her co-workers over the fiasco with Bobby.

Mentally willing herself to calm down, she stood for brief seconds at the door, considering what she was about to do. If for nothing else, she realized, she needed to get away to think about her life and its direction without any interruptions.

Locking the door behind her, she took the stairs quickly. Without a backward glance, she got into her car and drove off.

Keith had called Cienna's cell phone repeatedly. He'd called her apartment more than that. He didn't know where she could be. Why hadn't he walked out of Charles' office sooner? Why hadn't he gone with her? He paced the floor in her office, wondering where she could possibly be. He remembered her parents lived in New York, but where? She had never told him where they lived exactly. He flipped through the Rolodex on her desk in search of a number for her parents or an address. He'd try there next.

He had just found the number when he heard loud voices coming from down the hall. He looked down at his watch. It was almost eight o'clock. Who would still be in the office at this time of night?

Getting up from the chair, he moved to the door and looked up and down the hallway. He saw no one, but he still heard voices and walked in their direction. When he neared Charles' office, he heard an angry woman's voice.

"You thought you could just pass me on to your friend and be done with me. But I told you I had plans. I told you what I wanted."

Keith recognized the voice and moved closer to the door.

"You're insane. I told Lee you were crazy. I told him you weren't worth the money he wasted on condoms," Charles taunted. "You were just an employee. I told you that from the beginning."

"Oh, yeah, that's right. An employee at both of your businesses. Your highly respectable and successful law firm as well as your financially flourishing escort service."

Those words had Keith halting just before entering the office.

"You needed the money, remember?" Charles told her.

"Yeah, I needed the money. But I wanted more. I wanted love." Her voice cracked.

"Who the hell did you think was going to fall in love with you?"

"Somebody has to love me, sooner or later somebody has to love me."

The woman was crying. Locked to that spot beside the door, Keith couldn't believe what he had just heard, nor the implications it had.

"Get the hell out of my office before I call the police! You make me sick!" Charles bellowed.

"Oh, I make you sick now?" the female laughed. "A few months ago, I did things you wished your wife would do to your sorry ass. I made you a very happy man. You remember that?"

"You weren't the only employee I slept with," Charles informed her.

"No, but not only did I sleep with you, I slept with your partner, and along the way I made you both a shitload of money. Then you both decided to get cute and push me to the side. You both figured you were ready to move on."

"What the hell do you think you're going to do with that gun?"

"Your poor unsuspecting wife is about to become a very rich, very embarrassed lady. You see, I've already sent press releases to all the papers and TV stations. First thing tomorrow morning, you and Lee will be exposed for the cheating, scandalous characters you are."

"You didn't," he whispered.

"Oh, yes I did. And there's nothing you can do to stop it."

At the mention of a gun, Keith ran to the nearest cubicle and dialed 9-1-1. He hastily explained to the 9-1-1 operator that someone was being threatened with a gun, gave the location, dropped the phone onto the desk, leaving the line open, and rushed back toward Charles' office. They were still arguing, and their angry shouting reached his ears.

"I don't want to hear another word! I tried to give you the benefit of the doubt, I tried to make it work."

"Is that why you tried to seduce me earlier today? Because you thought that would make it better. You're stupider than I thought."

"No, I'm not as stupid as you thought."

Just as Keith pushed the door open to intervene, the gun exploded.

The woman turned to leave and saw Keith frozen in the doorway. She pointed the gun at him.

"Inside." She motioned with her head. "I won't hesitate to shoot you, too."

A glance into her wild eyes, and he raised his hands. "No problem. I'll just see about Charles." He edged closer to Charles' desk.

The woman laughed bitterly. "You do that. I've got unfinished business to take care of." She backed to the door and pulled it closed behind her. Then Keith heard the lock click firmly into place.

Taking a deep breath, he turned to Charles. He tore his eyes away from the ghastly head wound and checked for a pulse. There was none. He shook his head in disbelief. And what was worse, this might not be the end of it. What had she meant by "unfinished business"?

Tired and exhausted after several hours of conversation with the police, Keith went back to Cienna's office to claim the number he'd found just before the unthinkable had happened. He needed to find Cienna, now more than ever.

In the past few hours, he'd learned some incredible facts. The man he'd once looked up to, he now despised. In a couple of hours, the news would air, and all the dirty laundry of Raleigh Simms and Charles Benton would be exposed. RES stock would plummet, and all chances for the contract with the state would go down the drain. As for Benton and King, Keith wasn't sure what would become of the twenty-year-old firm or its employees.

But at this moment, he didn't really care about any of that. He simply wanted to find Cienna and hold her in his arms. She'd once told him he needed a woman who would know where to touch him when he was stressed. He was beyond being stressed and he needed her desperately.

CHAPTER TWENTY

"I'm sorry, baby, she didn't say where she was going. Just that she'd be gone for a few days," Adelle Turner told Keith sadly. Her heart went out to the man. He sounded so distressed. Cienna hadn't told her what had happened that made her feel as though she had to run away, but she instinctively knew it had something to do with the man on the other end of the phone.

"Thank you, Mrs. Turner," he said gravely. "If she should happen to get in touch with you, would you please ask her to call me?"

"I sure will." She'd do more than ask her. What could possibly be going on in that child's mind? Running away never solved anything. "I'm sure she's alright, maybe just needed some space."

"Yeah, maybe." He said his goodbyes and hung up the phone.

Space. She'd needed space from him. She'd run away from him. He wanted to be angry, he wanted to yell and scream, but who would hear him? Who would even care?

Keith drove to her apartment. Even though her mother had said she was gone for a few days, he climbed out of his car and went to the door anyway. Maybe, just maybe, she'd still be there. He pressed the buzzer with all his pent-up anger. The sound blared through the neighborhood like a broken horn. Someone, probably one of her neighbors, tired of hearing the annoying sound finally gave in and sounded the buzzer that signaled the opening of the downstairs door.

Grateful for annoyed neighbors, he took the steps two at a time. His heart was pounding with fury as he approached her door. How long would this back-and-forth game go on between them? He knew one thing: He loved Cienna Turner, but he was getting damn tired of chasing her.

Before Cienna, he had never had to chase a woman in his life, but in the last couple of weeks that's all he'd been doing. First, he'd all but begged for a date. Like a schoolboy, he'd pleaded with her to sleep with him. Now he was at her door again. For what? To make her see that they were meant to be together. To beg her to stop being a ninny and get with the program.

This was ridiculous. She wanted him, and he knew it. But she couldn't bring herself to admit it. What kind of woman was she? She had such brash confidence in the office, when she could hide behind the title of counselor. But when she was stripped of the title, what kind of woman was she? The kind of woman he had fallen hopelessly in love with, he thought. Resting his forehead on the door, he felt all the anger seep out of him.

"Cienna," he whispered. His heart ached for this woman that he couldn't seem to reach. He had sensed that there was something else going on, something that she hadn't wanted to share with him. He'd been willing to wait for her to tell him when she was ready, but now he wondered if she'd ever be ready.

Did she really trust him so little that she couldn't open up to him? She had shared her body with him, but she wouldn't share her soul. Why? Depleted, he was about to turn and go back down the stairs when he saw a piece of paper on the floor outside her door. Stooping, he picked up the paper, which turned out to be some sort of brochure. Opening it, he felt waves of relief wash over him. Seneca Falls.

Pulling into the newly paved driveway, Cienna stared at the building before her. The Driftwood Inn was a tall, colonial building with stark white columns. Boasting a gorgeous view of Cayuga Lake, the bed-and-breakfast was nestled in the center of the Finger Lakes Region of Upstate New York.

Mionne had suggested the place to her a few months ago after a particularly vigorous trial. Cienna hadn't needed it then, but she definitely needed it now.

She had made reservations on her cell phone while she drove. Luckily, it was the beginning of their down season, and they still had rooms available. She'd called her mother to tell her that she'd be away for a few days. She didn't want her to worry, but knowing Adelle, she'd worry anyway.

She hadn't called Keith.

After checking in, she went immediately to her room. Stark white with large windows, it was spacious enough to accommodate two queen-sized four-poster beds, a heavy oak dresser and a comfortable looking sofa.

Going to the window, she allowed herself to be sucked in by the magnificent scenery. Lake Cayuga glistened a short distance away, its surface rippled by the gentle breeze. The sun had just set, and copper lights danced over the water's dark surface.

Letting her forehead rest on the cool glass of the window, Cienna closed her eyes in an effort to clear her mind. "What now?" she murmured.

The room gave no answer, but its silence offered refuge.

Keith drove like a man on a mission. He hadn't even stopped at his apartment before getting on the road headed towards Seneca Falls. She was there, he knew it; he could feel it.

The weight of the world seemed to rest on his shoulders. What was he going to do when he found her? He wasn't quite sure. All he knew was that he loved her, and finding her was of the utmost importance.

But she needed to love him, too. She needed to trust him. He wasn't a fool; he knew he couldn't make her feel any of these emotions. She'd have to come to them on her own.

But how long would that take?

Cienna lay in bed amongst several fluffy white pillows. She hadn't slept well; thoughts of Keith had constantly invaded her mind. The more she pushed him aside, the more he barged in. And the worst part was, she didn't know what to do about it.

She loved him, she knew she did, but admitting it to herself wasn't really the problem, was it? Once she said it aloud, once he knew and once everyone else knew, the trouble would begin.

She frowned at her thoughts. She wasn't quite sure whether she was still employed at Benton and King, so the problem of the office finding out might not even be a problem anymore. And whether or not she loved him was no longer a question. No, her dilemma was where to go from here.

Keith hadn't followed her out of Charles' office. He hadn't stood behind her when she refused to continue working on Simms' case. Did this truly mean that his feelings for her only went as far as the bedroom? Was he so focused on his career that he couldn't put her first? That had been her first assumption. Dismally she remembered telling him that *her* career came before personal involvement. Had that remark come back to haunt her?

The sun was extra bright this morning and glared through the windows with a fierce intensity. Pulling the covers over her head, she groaned. More than anything, she wished she could stay under these covers until all her troubles were gone. But she knew that wasn't possible. She had to deal with her situation.

Rising from the bed, she went into the lavish bathroom and indulged in a long, hot bubble bath. When she emerged, her skin was wrinkled and tingly from the heat. But her muscles were relaxed, and her mind was calm. Not clear, but calm.

She stepped into an old pair of jeans and slipped on an oversized sweatshirt in preparation for her day. *How else did one prepare to do nothing?* she wondered. She'd never done nothing before. Pulling her hair back and securing it with a scrunchie, she donned an old Yankees cap and was finally ready to do nothing.

As she stepped onto the porch, the brisk fall breeze that crackled through the air with unfamiliar scents invigorated her. Inhaling deeply, she struck out in an easterly direction. Passing several small estates right on the water, she wondered what type of people lived there. The homes looked like places where a person could be alone with their thoughts. Wasn't that what she wanted?

No, she admitted to herself, she really wanted to run away from her thoughts. Run from her fears. She knew that was the coward's way out, but who the hell cared if she was a coward?

She did, she thought sadly.

A flock of ducks flew overhead, squawking and flapping their wings. Flying south for the winter, she thought idly. She wished she were so free.

She had to get a handle on her life.

Keith. Her feelings for him had brought her here, her confusion about where their relationship was going. The thought of another betrayal from another man had sent her into an emotional spiral. She had assumed that Charles would side with his friend, but had expected Keith to back her up. But he hadn't. It seemed she was just another woman to him.

Another woman, she thought sadly. Her heart felt heavy, and her throat ran dry as she thought of Keith with another woman. Maybe the woman who had been calling him at the office, refusing to let their relationship end. Cienna cringed. She wouldn't be able to stand it. She knew it with a certainty. No matter how strong people thought she was, she knew she really wasn't.

But another woman wasn't really the problem this time. No, this time she had been betrayed by a man's career instead of his lust for another woman.

Yet in spite of everything, she couldn't forget the serious look in his eyes when he talked of their being together, how alive she felt when she was with him. *And* he was damn good in bed! She smiled at that thought. She had to concede that of all the lovers she had ever had, Keith Page definitely ranked number one. And she had run from him.

Pausing at the end of a dock, she sat and let her legs dangle over the edge. The water rippled lightly beneath the breeze, and she shivered. Maybe she should have brought a jacket. If Keith were here, he'd keep me warm, she thought.

She had to shake her head at her own stupidity. It seemed that the answer was just sitting in the palm of her hand waiting for her to take hold of it. She was in love with Keith Page.

And despite the fact that he hadn't acted in the way she thought he should have, she believed that Keith Page loved her, too. That had scared her. That was why she'd spent the last few weeks fighting Keith at every turn, denying what he already knew was there. Though what had happened with Bobby had definitely scarred her, she wasn't beyond repair, and Keith wasn't Bobby. He'd proven it over and over again. The drama about people at work finding out about her and Keith had all been a smoke screen to avoid admitting to herself that she was falling in love with Keith Page.

For a successful attorney, she realized, she wasn't the brightest character when it came to relationships. She smiled to herself as she reached a decision. She would go back. She had to go back. To Keith.

Fleeing, Mionne's mind was in turmoil.

Everything was ruined; she'd gambled again and lost again. Tears stung her eyes and burned the back of her throat as she thought of the revenge she would shortly take on the person who had pretended to be her friend.

All her life, she'd beensecond best; first, to her mother, whose husband had crept into her room every night from the time she turned thirteen until the day she left home; and finally, to the woman who had pretended to befriend her three years ago, deceiving her with smiles and compliments. She'd trusted Cienna until her last boyfriend met Cienna at an office party and began making a fool out of himself to impress her. Cienna had pretended not to be interested, but Mionne knew better. Beautiful women were all the same; they all wanted trophies.

Then Mionne had set her sights on bigger and better things. Charles, the managing partner of Benton and King, had willingly taken her into his bed until she'd begun to push for something more. Then he'd politely informed her that he no longer required her services and had passed her along to his friend and business partner.

Lee had been nice to her, giving her choice assignments and paying her big bucks to share her talents with the influential men of the City Planning Board. Then he'd decided to make her exclusively his. She thought that she'd finally found the man of her dreams, that Lee was going to make her his wife. Then he'd changed.

She'd gone to her friend, to Cienna, because she'd thought she would understand. But she hadn't. Instead, Cienna had taken Lee's side. She had sided against her friend.

She was tired, so very tired of the people she loved betraying her, hurting her. It was their turn to hurt now. She was determined to make all of them feel the same pain she had. Lee had felt it. Charles had felt it. And now, now Cienna would feel it, too.

Cienna was about to turn in for the night. In the morning she would return to the city and to Keith. She'd tell him how she felt and hope he'd understand. Her job, her career, well, she'd deal with that too. But she'd deal with Keith first because for the first time in her life she believed that she could have it all, a successful career and a flourishing personal life. She would have it all with Keith.

Clad only in her nightgown, she closed the book she'd been staring blankly at for the past hour and clicked off the light on the stand next to the couch. Moving toward the door to double-check the locks, she was startled by a brisk knock.

Curious, she moved closer to the door and whispered, "Who is it?"

"Hey Cee, it's me, Mionne."

What is she doing here? Cienna wondered as she clicked the lock and opened the door. And how did she know where she was?

"What are you doing here?" Cienna asked when she and Mionne stood face-to-face.

"I just needed someone to talk to. You know, a friend." Mionne stepped into the room. She didn't bother to wait for an invitation. She was sure she wouldn't receive one, after the way she'd treated Cienna over the last few weeks. "Girl, so much has been going on. I just don't know where to start."

Mionne was across the room plopping her voluptuous body onto the sofa before Cienna could say another word. Cienna closed the door, confused by Mionne's sudden arrival and even more so by the friendly air she was attempting to exude. Something was going on, she thought. She would proceed with caution.

"So you came to me?" Taking slow steps toward the couch, Cienna tried to read Mionne's true intentions, but she'd just turned out the light and the dim light cast by the television masked Mionne's face cleverly.

"Yeah, when I tried your apartment and you weren't there, I figured you'd come here. Before things got crazy, you kept saying you were going to take the time to come up here for a few days. So I came on a hunch." Mionne scooped up the remote and flicked the channels. "I guess my hunch was right."

"I guess so." Cienna circled the couch and took a seat at the table near the window. "So what's up?" she asked tentatively.

"What's going on with you and Keith? You've been huddled up in that office a lot lately."

"We're working on a case together." Cienna didn't offer any more information than that. Although she couldn't quite put her finger on it, something about Mionne's presence here unsettled her. Mionne had barely spoken to her in the last two weeks, and just yesterday she'd made that weird statement about her time coming to an end. Cienna folded her hands in her lap and watched the woman on the couch carefully, trying to gauge her attitude, her reason for being there.

"Oh, working a case. That's good." Mionne nodded in Cienna's direction before turning her attention back to the television.

An hour passed with Mionne chattering endlessly and Cienna either nodding in agreement or giving some nonchalant comment until she simply couldn't stand it anymore.

"What are you really doing here, Mionne? And don't give me that crap about friendship and needing to talk to someone, because we both know that's a bunch of bull." Cienna stood to show Mionne that she was getting tired of this charade.

Mionne paused a moment, her fingers poised over the buttons on the remote. They had watched everything from sitcoms to the home and gardening channel in the time since Mionne had gotten there. Now, some infomercial with Vanessa Williams was on. "You know, counselor," Mionne chuckled, "you've always been smarter than me."

Gliding her fingers along the buttons on the remote, she kept her eyes fixed on the screen.

"Smarter than me, prettier than me, stronger than me. You're just better than me, period."

Cienna's mind raced as she tried to make sense of Mionne's words.

"But this time, your beauty, which I might add is suffering as a result of all that's going on in your life right now, is not going to save you."

For the first time since Mionne's arrival, Cienna felt the unfamiliar prickling of fear. Standing in front of the window, she wrapped her arms around her midsection as if she could shield herself from whatever was about to occur. "What are you talking about?"

"You should have just gone along with him, and you wouldn't have gotten into such a mess. He only wanted to have a little fun with you," she began. "You see, that's always been one of your problems. You don't know how to have fun. Me, on the other hand, I know how to have fun. I know how to do whatever it is a man wants me to do in order to please him."

"Mionne, you're confusing me. I don't know what you're talking about. Who wanted to have fun with me?" Cienna's voice was a hoarse whisper, and her hands clutched the material of her nightgown tightly.

"Lee was a good man. At least he was until you came into the picture. You see, I went back in my mind and tried to figure out when it was that things changed between me and Lee, and I came back to the night in the club." Mionne changed the channel on the television again. "I saw him come over and talk to you. I thought maybe he knew you through Charles or from work. But then when I saw him grab your hand when you got up, I knew something else was going on. I tried to ignore it. Lee liked women. All sorts of women, he liked them all. While you were looking for me, I reminded him how I could make him forget all about everything, and after I dropped you off, I met him at the Radisson."

Cienna stared blankly at the woman she had called a friend. The man Mionne called Lee, the man who was her boyfriend, was none other than Raleigh Simms. Shock held her silent, fear held her still.

CHAPTER TWENTY-ONE

"Lee took care of his women. I worked for him and Charles for more than two years, and I was Lee's favorite for almost seven months. Yup, for seven months I didn't have any other clients. It was just Lee and me." Mionne shifted a bit on the sofa, lifting one plump leg onto the pillows. "Then he saw you. A few days after we were at the club, he called and asked me how I knew, you. I told him. Then the next thing I knew you were working on a case involving him. And I, after seven months, got another client."

Every word Mionne said went through Cienna's mind at a rapid pace. If Lee were Raleigh, then why hadn't Mionne said something before? What kind of special work did she do for Lee and Charles? She had said Charles, hadn't she? Mionne had been Charles' secretary for three years, since coming to the firm. But that didn't explain the work she did for both him and Simms. Cienna was confused. She didn't like the way this story was unraveling. She didn't like it one bit.

"I saw the client right downstairs in our building that day. Then I came back to the office and threw up. I was in love with Lee. I'd told him that, and he had said we'd be together forever. Yet, he'd made an appointment for me. He shared me with another man and didn't think twice about it."

At that, Cienna found her voice. And although her insides clenched and retracted, she spoke loudly enough for Mionne to hear her. "What kind of work did you do for them?" She was afraid of the answer, but she had to know. This all seemed like a really, really cruel joke to her, and she needed concrete answers to prove to her it was real. That she had actually been in the midst of something she'd known nothing about.

Mionne laughed. "Poor little Cienna. Are you that naïve? Do you really believe that all that money came strictly from Charles' and Lee's professions? Let me enlighten you. For the past twenty years, they were partners in one of the city's largest escort services." When Cienna only stared at her, Mionne continued. "They pimped women, Cienna, to their friends, their colleagues, politicians they wanted to get on their side, you name it. They had about fifty women in their employ. And just recently, they stepped into the twenty-first century by adding a few men to the roster. Yeah, it was very lucrative for them both."

"So you were like a...a prostitute?" Cienna stumbled over the words.

"Call it what you like," she waved her hand. "I like sex. It's that simple." Mionne shrugged and moved along another couple of channels.

Cienna backed up until the crooks of her knees hit the chair she had previously sat in. Because they threatened to buckle and leave her lying in the floor, her legs bent appropriately, and she took a seat again. Flabbergasted was not enough to explain how shocked she was. She'd thought she'd known Mionne. This was a person she had called her friend. So her friend was a prostitute? She couldn't believe it.

She looked across the dark room at the woman absently playing with the remote. Her hair pinned up in a neat French roll, earrings dangling to her neck, she wore a black pantsuit and flat black shoes. Who would have ever figured her for a prostitute? Cienna sure hadn't. "But why, why would you do such a thing? I mean, you're intelligent; you've got great clerical skills. You could have been anything you wanted."

Mionne's head snapped in Cienna's direction, and she gave her an icy glare. She was damned tired of Cienna's condescending tone with her. It took everything in her to keep her from wrapping her hands around that pretty little neck this instant and squeezing the life out of her. Who was she to tell her what she could have been? She didn't know her. She didn't know anything about her. And she didn't care. "I'm not like you, Cienna." The words said so simply held more meaning to Mionne than Cienna could have ever imagined.

It was the first time in three years she had been able to admit that she wasn't like Cienna. As much as she wanted the statement to be false, it wasn't; and that fact stung. There had been times in the past three years that she'd thought she could be just like Cienna, if she only tried. She'd start a diet, buy new clothes and try to talk and think as Cienna would. But nothing had changed. Charles had treated her just the same, and so had Lee.

"I'm different. I've always been different," Mionne said. She remembered her mother telling her that as early as when she was eleven years old. Her mother's husband had confirmed it each night he'd snuck into her room. And every man she'd ever slept with since then had always claimed she was different from any woman they had ever met. Mionne hadn't yet figured out if they meant that in a good or bad way.

"Lee wanted you. He wanted you badly. Charles knew it, but he didn't care. He just wanted you and Keith to get Lee off those charges so that the big deal would go through. See, Benton and King was going to profit substantially from that deal. Charles and Lee were going to close up shop on their other little business venture after it. But you were supposed to be more than Lee's lawyer. When you didn't cooperate, you messed up the whole plan."

"Oh, my God," Cienna whispered. She couldn't believe what she was hearing. Charles had betrayed her. "I don't understand. Why me?" She hugged her arms around her waist leaning over slightly, rocking back and forth trying to console herself, trying to make this all make sense.

"Lee was intrigued by you. Lee was a very important man in this city, a very hot commodity. But you brushed him off. You didn't care who or what he was, you just didn't want him. You only wanted Keith."

Cienna thought of Keith. She thought of what he was going to say, how he was going to react, when she told him all this. Her mind began to clear. They had used her. Men had once again used her. Charles wanted the deal to go through, and Lee needed one last conquest; and she was the key to it all. So why put Keith on the case, too? To throw people off, she guessed. It was never about offering both the male and female perspective. They'd thought that Cienna would sleep with Lee, and Keith would win the case. She felt bile rise in her throat and struggled to keep it at bay.

"So after I cleared Simms' name, what was supposed to happen? Charles and Simms would go off and accept that city contract, rake in mega-bucks and disband their little brothel?" She felt her blood pumping rapidly through her veins and her words came out crisp. She didn't appreciate being a pawn in their little game.

"Something like that."

Cienna sat straight up in the chair staring at Mionne. How could she have allowed herself to be used so viciously? What drove a woman to stoop so low? "I don't understand, Mionne. Why would you let Lee or Raleigh or whatever you want to call him treat you like that? Why would you let any man treat you like that?" Cienna wanted desperately to understand. Maybe it was because she respected herself and her body far too much to allow herself to be used and discarded that way. Maybe it was because she was already disgusted with men who only looked at a woman's body and thought of how they could benefit from it. But if the truth be told, she was more puzzled by how Mionne could have continued undetected in this charade for three years. How she could have befriended her, confided in her, socialized with her and never known the type of woman she really was.

"Because I like it. I like the attention, and I love the sex. You see, Cienna, not all of us are blessed with your brain and sexy body. Some of us have to take what we can get, when we can get it. And that's what I did." Abruptly Mionne stood, dropping the remote to the floor. She reached for her purse that she'd dropped on the chair when she first came in and began to rummage through it.

"Does that make you happy? Does that satisfy you?" Cienna's heart began to ache for the woman she'd called her friend.

"Hell, yeah, it makes me happy. Somebody pays my rent and takes care of all my bills, and he does everything a boyfriend should do."

"Except respect you," Cienna whispered.

"We can't always get exactly what we want in life, Cienna. I had to learn that the hard way." For a moment, Mionne's hand stilled in her purse, and she stared at Cienna blankly. "When I was a little girl, I wanted my mother to love me like she loved my sister, but she never did. I wanted her husband to stop hurting me, but he never did. When I grew up, I realized that I was the only one who could get me what I wanted. So that's what I did. Men are funny creatures, Cienna. You give them what they need most, and they'll give you whatever you want. You think I'm a prostitute, but I call myself a businesswoman."

"A businesswoman who got burned this time around." Cienna watched Mionne's whole body stiffen at her words and bravely continued. "You messed up this time. In the line of business you're in, you should know it doesn't pay to get personal, but you did this time. You fell in love with Simms. You fell in love with the power he exuded, the money he flashed before you, and you thought, 'Maybe this one is meant for me.'" When Mionne didn't move, Cienna stood from her chair and stared at her eye-to-eye. "But then he got tired of you and found himself another whore to hang on his every word. That hurt you, didn't it? You wanted him to marry you. Yeah, he'd promised you would be together forever, but he didn't mean as husband and wife. No, he meant he didn't mind screwing you for the rest of your life while he and his wife lived happily ever after. He played you, and it was all your fault for being stupid enough to believe that you were ever anything more to him than just another whore."

Mionne's hand shook as it clamped around the cool metal of her gun. Dropping her purse to the floor, she pointed the gun toward Cienna, her finger sliding easily around the trigger.

Cienna gasped. Even in the dimly lit room, she could see the gun clearly. Her fists clenched at her sides and her heart thumped heavily in her chest. This wasn't happening. This could not be happening.

Mionne raised her arm slowly until the gun aimed directly at Cienna's head. "I'm sick and tired of you preaching to me, Cienna." Mionne pronounced every word distinctly. "You're not perfect. Remember, you told me how that guy Bobby played you." In light of the full moon coming through the window, Mionne saw the flicker of memory cross Cienna's face. "Yeah, I'm not the only one who can get played. It happened to you, too. As a matter of fact, it happened to you twice. Keith just played you again. So you can get down off your high horse. "

At the mention of his name, Cienna felt a stab of hurt. Keith had not played her. It hadn't been just about sex with them. She struggled with Mionne's words because she was still trying to convince herself of this fact. Cienna tried to remain calm. Falling apart wasn't going to help in this situation; a clear head was the only thing that was going to save her life.

"Yeah, he wanted you in his bed. I heard him and Charles talking about it. And he got you there. Now look at you, hiding out like a wounded animal. If you would just look at it like I do, you wouldn't be so upset right now. You wanted to sleep with him, so you did. It's as simple as that. Sex is as simple as that."

"I don't sleep with men for money. And I definitely don't sleep with married men," Cienna said as her only retort to Mionne's allegations.

"So what if he's married! She can't love him like I can!" Mionne yelled. "He doesn't love her anyway, not the way he loves me. Hell, she won't even go down on him," she sucked her teeth. "Now what kind of wife is that?"

"Apparently the kind he wants, or he would've left her long ago. There is more to love than blowjobs, Mionne." Cienna's remark earned her a nasty scowl from Mionne, and her heartbeat quickened as Mionne closed the space between them.

"Don't get smart with me, I'm holding all the cards now. I'm tired of talking anyway! Let's go!" She flicked the gun, and Cienna didn't hesitate to move in the direction Mionne had indicated.

Cienna reached to open the door. Maybe out in the open, she could escape. Mionne's extra forty pounds would surely slow her down. Then she remembered that bullets travel at the speed of light.

CHAPTER TWENTY-TWO

Pulling up in front of the cozy-looking house, Keith prayed that some small part of Cienna would be glad that he had come.

Once he found the brochures, he hadn't hesitated about making the trip. So, she thought she needed time away, space. Well, he didn't intend to give her either one. Relationships floundered with too much of either, and he had no intention of letting that happen. Besides, he needed to be the one to tell her what had happened the previous night.

He loved her, and it was high time she knew it. This was not the way an adult relationship progressed. He had never really been a part of a relationship before, but he was sure this wasn't how it worked. There should be closeness, trust, friendship, all in accordance with intimacy.

He realized there was something that was keeping Cienna from loving him, and he wanted to know what it was. If he planned to spend the rest of his life with her, which he did, he needed to know what he was up against.

It took fifty dollars and his gold money clip to find out what room she was in. The small round man at the front desk might have looked like a geek, but he was no pushover.

Taking the stairs two at a time, Keith had to struggle to hold his roaring emotions in check. In just a minute, they'd be face-to-face. In just a minute, he'd tell her how he felt about her. He'd hold her in his arms. He'd kiss her lips. He'd…

The door opened abruptly.

Cienna stared at Keith, eyes wide with shock, heart leaping for joy. From behind her, Mionne cursed, pushing the gun deeper into her back.

Normally the sight of Cienna alone had his blood boiling. Noting the skimpy nightgown she wore, he should have been on his knees panting. Instead, the fist of fear gripped his heart as he recognized Mionne standing close behind her.

"Ladies," he nodded stiffly. "Where are you off to at this time of night?" Keith inquired, saying the first thing that came to his mind.

"Oh, Keith, I'm surprised to see you here." Moving her eyes fiercely in Mionne's direction, she tried to alert him to the dangerous situation she thought he was unaware of. But Keith already had his gaze intent on Mionne.

"Come in," Mionne commanded. She pulled Cienna to the side, revealing the gun jammed into her spine.

Keith could still hear her voice as she'd argued with Charles, the single gunshot that had killed him. He quickly moved forward into the room.

Mionne shoved Cienna into Keith and pointed the gun toward the couple. "You showed up at the wrong time, pretty boy."

Cienna tumbled into Keith's arms, but after a momentary embrace, he pushed her behind him. His own heart hammered in his chest as he shielded her from the weapon.

Mionne's expression was crazed. That worried Keith, because he knew all too well what she was capable of. His mind worked furiously as he tried to figure out the safest way to save them both.

Cienna's hands tightly gripped Keith around the waist. He felt her fingers compressed against his navel and an idea crossed his mind. With very slow, very careful movements, he eased a hand over one of hers, moving it downward until it rested at his pocket.

"So this is how it's going to end?" Keith kept his eyes steady on Mionne as he guided Cienna's hand into his pocket, praying that the dimly lit room would conceal their actions.

"You should have just stayed away from her. She's bad luck, can't you see? But everybody's fooled by her pretty face. She's not as perfect as you think." Mionne grinned. Although her words were steady and clear, her hands shook as she held the gun.

"So now you'll just get rid of both of us?" he asked just as Cienna's fingers wrapped around his cell phone.

Cienna's heart skipped a beat as she realized what Keith was doing. She slowly slid her hand with the phone from his pocket. When the phone was behind Keith's back, she pressed the call button with shaky fingers.

"You might as well come from behind him. I have enough bullets in here for the both of you!" Mionne yelled.

Cienna dialed 9-1-1 before closing her fist around the small phone. Though she'd originally ridiculed the miniature size of the Nokia 3560, at this very moment she was thankful it was so tiny and easily concealed. She prayed the police would track the signal in time.

Cienna stepped partially out from behind Keith. "This is ridiculous, Mionne. You'll never get away with it. Once our bodies are found, there will be an investigation, and eventually they'll find you."

"Please, by the time they get a clue that I'm involved, I'll be long gone. I've got a nice little piece of change stashed away, and there's an island out there with my name on it." Mionne held on to the gun, shifting slightly as she moved a little closer to Cienna and Keith.

"You'll be wanted for four murders, they're going to be hot on your trail, so unless you can manage to get out of the country tonight, you're going to get caught," Keith added.

"Whatever. You and Ms. Thang should say your goodbyes now." Mionne aimed directly at Keith's head.

Cienna quickly spoke. "Is it really worth it? I mean, you already said that Lee was finished with you, and since it appears you no longer work for Benton and King, I assume Charles has tired of you as well. Why don't you just cut your losses and head out of town?" Cienna prayed that she could stall long enough for the police to get there. Keith's arrival had seemingly pushed Mionne a little closer to the edge.

Mionne laughed. "Charles and Lee are not my concern anymore. Actually, I would have already been out of town except for one more thorn in my side that needed to be removed." Mionne's eyes rested on Cienna.

"I thought we were friends." Cienna's voice was low, her eyes searching Mionne's for some semblance of the woman she'd known. "I don't understand."

Keith spoke before Mionne could answer. "There's nothing to understand, Cienna. They were all corrupt. Charles, Simms, Mionne, all of them.

They had things going on that none of us were aware of."

"I wasn't corrupt. At least not in the beginning. I just wanted a normal relationship," Mionne responded. She blinked and focused on her next two victims. Keith was holding Cienna close against his chest. Mionne's hand began to shake.

When Lee had sat at his desk smirking at her, laughing at her, pulling the trigger had been easy. With Charles, his blatant arrogance had pushed her beyond the brink. But with Cienna, something was holding her back. Something that remained in the dark recesses of her mind was preventing her from pulling the trigger. And now, Keith had stepped into the picture. He'd never done anything to her. But it was too late to reconsider; she needed to finish what she'd started.

"What was normal about your boss hiring you to be a secretary and pimping you out to his friends?" Cienna asked incredulously.

"It wasn't like that," Mionne wailed. "We were supposed to be exclusive!"

"Yeah, exclusively sick!" Keith murmured.

For that remark, Mionne moved her hand a few inches to the left, firing a single shot into the wall just above Cienna and Keith.

"Just so you and your little tramp know I'm serious." Mionne cocked her head to the side as if re-thinking the situation. "Sit down!" she ordered.

Cienna was still trembling from the gunshot when Keith pulled her toward the sofa. As they passed her, Mionne chuckled. "That's right, Cienna, you need to be afraid. But look at it this way, at least you'll die in your lover's arms."

"What are you waiting for? If you're going to shoot us, go ahead and get it over with. This cat-and-mouse game is getting tiresome." Keith tried to use reverse psychology, praying it didn't backfire on him. He'd seen Mionne's hand shake, and her little shot into the wall instead of at the persons she claimed to want dead gave him the impression that she was a little unsure of her intentions.

"Oh, you're ready now? Just a few minutes ago, your woman thought she could talk me down." Mionne moved to the chair directly across from them, tired of being on her feet.

"No, we were trying to get answers," Keith informed her. "But now that I realize the only real answer is that you, Charles, Simms and whoever else was in on this scheme were all insane, I figure there's no use drawing this thing out."

Cienna stared at Keith in disbelief. She knew what he was up to but was afraid he would go over-board. She had been so stunned by the gunshot she'd dropped the cell phone. She was afraid to move now, so looking for it was out of the question. She prayed the connection was still linked to the police and that Mionne wouldn't spot the phone.

Cienna tried to reason with her once more. "Mionne, you've got to reconsider this. There's no way you're going to get away with it, and a premeditated double-murder is likely to get you the death penalty."

"I told you I won't get caught," Mionne responded. "Now do you want your bullet first, or would you like to watch your man go before you?"

"Why don't you do first whichever one of us you want gone the most?" Keith proposed.

"But if she does me first, then you'll suffer. I don't want you to suffer." Cienna turned her face to Keith, who took both her hands in his.

"I don't want you to suffer either, baby." Keith rubbed Cienna's hands, watching Mionne out of the corner of his eye. This scene was bothering her, and she fidgeted in the chair.

"Shut up! Both of you just shut the hell up! I'm in charge of this situation, and whoever catches the first bullet will be my choice!" she yelled.

"Well, hurry up and make your damned choice!" Keith roared.

"Or you could reconsider," Cienna added.

"I said shut up!" Mionne screamed.

"You really don't have to kill me," Cienna continued.

"You're going to go to jail for a really long time," Keith persisted.

"This is so stupid, they're really not worth it."

"Go ahead and throw your life away over men that never wanted you in the first place."

Mionne rocked back and forth in the chair harder and harder until tears streamed down her face and memories of the past flooded her. Her stepfather as he groaned on top of her, Charles as he told her she would never be good enough for him, Lee as he told her he'd never made her any promises...On and on the memories came, all of them telling her she was second-best. She'd held it in for so long, for almost twenty-five years. She couldn't stand it any longer.

Mionne opened her eyes and focused on the moon through the window. Cienna and Keith watched in horror as the hand holding the gun shifted. The finger on the trigger squeezed, and the single shot rang loud and clear.

Cienna screamed.

Keith jerked and cradled Cienna in his arms as Mionne's lifeless body slumped to the floor.

CHAPTER TWENTY-THREE

Seconds later, Keith and Cienna jumped at the sound of wood splitting. What was left of the front door fell away as uniformed officers, guns raised, entered the room.

With one look at them, Cienna sighed and fell back into Keith's arms. As much as she hated it, as much as she felt it demeaned her, she let loose the dam of emotions that had been welled up inside her for months, and she cried. Keith hugged her closely, afraid to let her go. The sobs seemed to take everything out of her. Her body jerked and convulsed as she emptied herself completely.

An hour later, another question and answer session was wrapped up. Keith was exhausted from the last two days. He'd witnessed a murder and a suicide and been held at gunpoint. And to top that off, he still hadn't done what he'd set out to do in the first place.

Cienna sat in a chair at the little table near the window. Her eyes puffy and red from crying, she looked as if she were about to fall over from fatigue. Her legs were crossed, and her arms were wrapped around her waist tightly. She answered the detective's questions with all the knowledge she had, but she couldn't go much farther, he could see it in her face. He hadn't told her about Simms and Charles yet. But he knew he had to. She'd find out as soon as they returned to the city.

The lead detective interrupted Keith's thoughts. "When are you leaving?"

Keith stood from the sofa to face the middle-aged man. "I'm not sure. We can't stay here tonight, so I need to find us a place to sleep." Keith looked around the room. Mionne's body had been removed only moments before. Blood stained the wall adjacent to the chair where she had taken her own life. No, they couldn't stay here.

"The manager said he's preparing another room for you now. I'd like to talk to you two again in the morning just to make sure we have everything." The detective folded his notepad and tucked it and his pen into his jacket pocket.

"That's fine. You know where to reach us." Keith extended his hand. His lips upturned slightly as the detective gave his hand a quick shake.

"Okay, boys let's move out," he yelled to his men.

Cienna remained seated.

When the room was empty, Keith walked over to the little table and took the chair across from her. "The manager is getting us another room. If you don't want to stay here at all, I understand, and I'll go find us someplace else to go."

"No," she answered quickly. Her eyes met his across the table and held. "Another room is fine. I don't feel like traveling just yet."

He nodded in agreement. "There's something else you need to know."

"Oh, Lord, please, I can't take another thing tonight, Keith, really I can't." Cienna shook her head, wishing that the simple motion could erase the last few hours, the last few weeks.

"I know it's been rough, baby, but there's more you need to know." Keith wanted so badly to touch her, to console her. But he was afraid of her reaction; he was afraid of the way she sat in that chair, so fragile, so beaten.

Cienna sighed. She closed her eyes and lifted her hands to the back of her neck attempting to massage away the tension that had built over the past weeks. It didn't work. "What is it?" When he remained quiet, she opened her eyes and turned to him again. "Keith?"

"Simms is dead. And so is Charles."

She gasped, one hand flying to her mouth. She wanted to cry, she thought that was what she should do, but she was all cried out. She wanted to feel pity, but after what Mionne had told her, she couldn't muster that emotion either. In the end, she just shook her head again. "How?"

"Mionne shot Charles. I'm guessing she shot Simms first, though. The cops in the city are running tests on the bullets to see if they were from the same gun."

"They both slept with her, they both used her," Cienna said quietly.

"I don't understand. They seemed so level, so normal."

"Everybody has their own version of normal, I've learned. Mionne said she started out working for Charles, not the firm, Charles' other business. Then I guess he decided to get a piece of her, and when he was done with her he passed her on to Simms."

"And when Simms saw you, he was finished with her." The pained expression on Cienna's face told him that she was blaming herself. To hell with how fragile she looked. He had to touch her. If she crumbled, he'd pick her up, but he needed to feel her next to him. He stood from his chair and walked until he stood in front of her before going down on his knees. "They were both sick." He spoke softly, taking her hands in his own.

"I just wish I'd never met Simms. I wish none of this had ever have happened." The tears she'd thought were dried and gone welled up and slid down her cheeks. "I thought Mionne was my friend. And I only tried to help her. I would never have hurt her deliberately, not like they did. But she hated me anyway. She hated me," Cienna sobbed.

Releasing her hands, he folded his arms around her, letting her head rest on his shoulder. "Sweetie, I think Mionne hated herself. She wasn't strong enough to be the woman that you are, and that made her angry. Unfortunately, she directed that anger toward you when she should have held herself accountable. I'm sorry this had to happen, too. I'm so sorry you've had to go through this." He rocked her gently, his heart swelling with love for her. All he had wanted to do was protect her, and he had fallen dismally short in that area.

Not that he was fool enough to believe that he could have prevented any of this from happening. He only wished he could have spared her some of the pain she was going through. He'd give her anything, he'd do anything to take the pain away, but he didn't know how to make her see that.

Keith heard someone clearing his throat behind him. He shifted and turned in the direction of the door, or what was left of the door.

"Ah, sir. We have another room ready for you and the lady." The thin young man stood just beyond the yellow tape and ripped wood looking at Keith, apparently confused.

"Thanks. Just leave the key over there on the table." Keith motioned his head toward the coffee table in the living room area.

"Sure." With a few quick strides, the young man left the key on the table and maneuvered his way out of the room.

"Baby, they have another room for us. Where's your stuff?"

Cienna dragged her hands over her eyes, sniffling and trying to get herself under control. "I'll get it, it's in the bedroom." She tried to stand, but her knees were wobbly, and she swayed to the side.

"Wait a minute, I can do it for you." Keith stood, catching her against his chest.

"No," she spoke adamantly. "I'll be fine." She pushed away from his grip and moved toward the back room on her own.

He watched her disappear through the doorway, wondering what it was going to take for her to finally trust him.

After a fretful night's sleep, a breakfast of toast and coffee and a long hot shower, Cienna finally emerged from the bedroom.

Keith stood at the window looking toward the river. She wondered what he was thinking, what he was feeling. She hadn't allowed him to sleep with her last night. She'd wanted to be alone. He'd seemed to understand. But then he always did. His back faced her now, all broad shoulders and muscled arms. She remembered how it had felt to have those arms wrapped tightly around her.

What was she doing? She had cursed herself as she tossed and turned throughout the night. Keith had come to rescue her, of that she was sure. But he'd looked as surprised as she was to see Mionne, so maybe a rescue wasn't his intent. Then what was? Why had he come here, and how had he found her? While her need for answers had burned in her mind, she couldn't seem to voice the questions. Last night had been horrible. Mionne's accusations and admissions had stunned her, leaving her bewildered and confused about the woman she had called a friend. Cienna still hurt for the woman who had felt she had no other choice than to take her life. She hurt for the desperate need to be wanted that would forever be unfulfilled for Mionne.

At the same time, she could relate to that need. After the incident with Bobby, Cienna had thought that she never wanted to be involved again. But the exact opposite was true. She wanted to be involved; she wanted to be loved. She was just afraid to trust that she deserved these things. Her previous dealings with men had tainted her view of what a real relationship had to offer.

She had admitted to herself only hours earlier that she was tired of living life in the shadow of uncertainty. She was tired of second-guessing her heart and trying to do the logical thing. She wanted someone to love and she wanted to love that someone in return. Her heart swelled with these emotions as she watched the man who had opened her eyes and claimed her heart.

Would he understand? Would he care? Even as she asked those questions, she knew the answers. Keith cared about her, of that much she was certain. As for the rest, it would come in time. If he didn't love her now, he would or she would move on. But she would no longer deny herself the opportunity to find out. She would no longer run from the chance to experience what true love could bring.

Keith sensed her presence and turned to see her staring at him. She looked better, stronger, he thought. Her hair was swept back into a ponytail, her bare feet peeked from beneath too-big sweat pants and the long t-shirt snuggled close to her unbound breasts. This was going to be harder than he'd thought. He needed to talk to her, to set the record straight. He was tired of playing games. He wanted her; he loved her. It was that simple. At least for him it was.

"Cienna, baby, this has got to stop. I don't know what you want from me, but I'm not going to go on this way. You have got to make up your mind about us, and you have got to do it fast."

She stood there staring at him. Something about her looked strange. Something about the way she watched him. "And don't look at me like that," he almost yelled. He knew the look. He'd worn it himself.

He'd given it to her on more than one occasion. But now was not the time. There were things he needed to get off his chest. Things he wanted to say to her.

"Like what?" she said innocently.

"You know like what. I don't even want to go there. We need to talk, and we need to talk right now."

Cienna licked her lips and wondered just how Keith would feel if she seduced him, right now, right in the middle of this beautiful room at the lake. Last night had been awful. The thought of losing him had been too much to bear, but she couldn't very well tell him that she loved him while he was seething with barely disguised anger. Making love would release some of that anger for him.

"You don't have anything to say?" He shouted this time. Her quietness, coupled with the look on her face, was quickly unmanning him.

"Not really." She walked over to him, never taking her eyes from his.

"Cienna, I told you we need to talk." He tried to ignore the sparks he saw flashing in her brown eyes. He'd seen those sparks before, when she'd been atop him, riding like the wind. He shook his head to clear the memory. Now was not the time.

Cienna placed her hands on his chest.

"Cienna?" he pleaded.

"I know my name, Keith. It really doesn't matter how many times you say it, I won't forget." As she began to unfasten the buttons of his shirt, his muscles tightened beneath her hands. He jerked. The muscles in his strong jaw clenched. She had him.

Her hands went to his zipper and found his burgeoning erection. She stroked him gently at first, then with more enthusiasm. "I want you, Keith. I want all of you. Now." Her voice was clear, her request simple.

Keith swallowed hard. *What was a man to do?*

With one last effort, he spoke. "Cienna, I really think…"

"You told me one time not to think, just let things go where they may. Why don't you take your own advice?" She slipped her tongue into his mouth.

"Be careful, Cienna, I'm not playing with you anymore," he said when she turned her attention to his neck.

"I know what I'm doing." She stepped back, reached for the hem of her shirt, and pulled it over her head. The cotton shirt quietly hit the floor.

Keith's mouth went dry, his eyes riveted to the heavy mounds bared before him. Her breasts were beautiful. Their fullness rested quietly against her body, their nipples puckering under his gaze.

Cienna hooked her thumbs beneath the elastic of the sweatpants and pulled them down and tossed them aside.

Keith hissed. *Lord, she hadn't been wearing a stitch of underwear.* She stood before him gloriously naked, giving him all she had. He would have been a fool not to take it. On shaky legs, he closed the space between them. Falling to his knees, he kissed her belly, lavishing her navel with his tongue, gripping her hips with a fierceness that rocked Cienna off her feet. She held on to his shoulders to steady herself. When he pushed her against the sofa table, she gripped the sides of the cherry wood to keep from knocking it over.

"Open your legs, Cienna. Let me in." He nudged her legs apart. "Wider," he urged. He inhaled the glorious scent of her arousal and stared at her femininity in awe. His mouth began to water. As if she were a delicacy, he dragged his tongue slowly, lavishly, between the folds of her vagina. A groan rumbled deep in his chest.

Cienna arched her back and held on for the ride. Three fingers replaced his tongue to massage the swollen flesh. Cienna gasped, and her nectar flowed urgently into his hand. Keith moaned with delight, "I love to taste you."

"Yes," she whispered. Holding his head firmly in place, she shook as spasms of ecstasy soared through her body.

Spreading her legs wider, he feasted on her like a starved animal, her essence quenching a thirst only she could satisfy. "So sweet," he murmured, "so damned sweet."

"Keith,"

"Yeah, baby, it's all mine. Tell me it's mine," he said. "Tell me!

"It's all yours, baby, it's all yours," she breathed.

Keith inserted one finger into her opening, and then another, watching as her expression changed with each thrust. His erection strained and poked through his open zipper. He stood abruptly, removing his fingers while she panted with pleasure. Instinctively,f her hands found the hem of his shirt and lifted it over the taut muscles of his arms, dropping it absently to the floor. His eyes holding hers, he lifted his fingers to his mouth and sucked each one until it was free of her nectar.

Her breath hitched as his lips found hers again. She could smell herself on his mouth and swooned into his arms.

He ravished her mouth, stroking, nipping, biting. His hunger for her soared through his body at top speed.

Cienna felt him fumbling to get his pants down. "Let me." She released her hold on him and moved to unfasten his pants. As she pulled his pants down, she lowered herself until his fullness was close to her mouth. Cupping his taut buttocks, she urged him forward, her tongue snaking out to touch the tip of his arousal. Keith gritted his teeth, and his hands grabbed at her hair, releasing it from the rubber band that bound it together. Then he raked his hands through the soft trestles.

"Damn!" Keith murmured. "You've got one great mouth, lady." His hips involuntarily moved against the ministrations of her mouth.

Wrapping her hand around his length, she pulled her head back until her mouth had fully released him. With passion-filled eyes, she glared up at him. "Tell me it's mine," she demanded as her tongue flicked quickly over the head of his arousal.

"Oh, God! It's yours, baby, it's yours. Damn! It's all yours." He lost his fingers in her hair as she continued her assault. "You keep this up, and you're going to be sadly disappointed," he warned.

"Does that mean you're ready for me?" Rising to face him, she feigned ignorance.

"Oh, yeah! Open up and let me in," he requested before his tongue plunged deep into her mouth. He kissed her the way he had kissed her tender cove, and Cienna almost whimpered in his arms. He lifted her and her legs snaked around his waist, clasping at the ankles to secure her position. His hands gripped her bottom, spreading her wider for his entrance. His long, hard shaft slid inside and claimed its home.

With thrust after glorious thrust, he gave her all he had, and she took all that she wanted. Still deep inside of her he walked over to the small round table that served as a kitchenette and laid her gently atop the strong oak.

He stared at her lying there, waiting for him patiently, lovingly. He had never loved anyone as he loved her. He loved every inch of her, and he could wait no longer to tell her so. "I love you, Cienna." He loved her with a gentleness that rocked her very soul. The strokes sounded through the room with a loud slurping sound that was music to Keith's ears. He threw his head back and enjoyed the warmth that caressed his shaft.

He heard her murmur something and blinked to clear his mind. "What?" He stopped mid-stroke.

"I said 'I love you, too,'" she told him as she reached for him.

He carefully leaned over her, not wishing to break the table, and kissed her gently.

"I love you," she said again.

"Good, because I don't plan on letting you go." Relief washed over him like a flood.

"Good, because I don't plan on letting you go either." Keith took her words and let them take him over the edge, but not before securing her passage to ecstasy right along with him.

Later, they lay in the queen-sized bed wrapped around each other after round three. Sweat glistened on each of their bodies, and they struggled to breathe normally again.

"Cienna, I want you to be sure. I mean, I know that it took you a while to come to this decision. I don't want all the emotions of last night to be what pushed you," he began.

"They didn't," she answered. "I just decided to let some things go."

"Some things like what?" Propped up on his elbow, he stared at her languid features. She looked like a woman well pleased and well loved. "You can tell me now," he prodded gently.

And she knew that she could. Finally, she could.

"A long time ago, I was involved with this guy that worked in the same building that I did. We had been dating for about a year when I heard rumors about him seeing a number of other women in the building. I tried to brush it off, chalking it up to simple gossip. Then one day, I came home and caught him. So I had to let him go. Needless to say, I was devastated. I trusted him, and he hurt me."

"I won't hurt you, Cienna." Lightly caressing her neck, he vowed it to her.

"I know you won't. But that's not all. You see, while we were dating, I devoted all my time to him and our relationship. I went out when he wanted to and where he wanted to. There were times that I had cases to summarize and transcripts to review, and I didn't do them, or I did a piss-poor job on them because I was either out late with him the night before or I had spent a long weekend with him and didn't even bother to go to work on Monday. I lost that job two weeks after I broke up with him."

"I'm sorry to hear that. But he was the jerk." Smoothing her eyebrows, he watched her intently. So this was what had stood between them. Some jackass that didn't appreciate what he had. Keith wanted to strangle the idiot, but the loss of Cienna Turner was punishment enough.

"Yeah, he was a jerk for cheating on me. But I was the jerk for not doing my job. That's why I decided I couldn't have both a relationship and work. That's why I fought my feelings for you so earnestly."

"So why are you with me now? What changed your mind?" he asked, needing desperately to know.

"Because I can't fight it anymore. Because you have erased all those feelings of hurt and disappointment. Being with you is right because it's what I want, and I'm going to work damn hard at this relationship thing so it doesn't fall apart. And I'll be a partner one day, because it's what I want and I'll work hard at that as well."

"We'll both work hard at this relationship thing. It's new to both of us. And for the partnership you want so badly, I'll work hard to support you in any way that I can, because I love you." He kissed her then, long, slowly and completely.

When his hands moved to her breasts, she felt a familiar tingling inside.

"We're going to wear each other out," she smiled.

"Nah, I'm full of energy. How about you?"

"I'm going to have to start working out to keep up." Curling her leg around his waist, she lifted her neck so he could nuzzle her closely.

"No, don't you change a thing. Don't you dare change a thing." He happily toyed with her nipple. "Cienna, are we okay now? I mean, with the job and the relationship, are we okay?" he asked cautiously.

Cupping his face in her hands, she marveled at the way he looked at her, with such obvious caring, such obvious love and trust. How could she have ever run from that? "Yeah, we're okay. But I'm not all that sure about our work status right now with everything that just happened." She hated to bring that up at this very moment but it was a part of their reality, their future.

"I was thinking that maybe we could open our own firm." He had thought of the idea after they'd been together on Saturday and hadn't planned on mentioning it to her for at least another month or so, but he figured since he had her in such a pliable mood, he'd go for it.

"Us who?" Cienna asked, incredulously.

"Me and you. We could call it 'Page and Page'." Settling himself comfortably inside her, he waited for her response.

"My last name's not Page." She was trying to concentrate on the words he spoke, but her mind was distracted by his thrusts, which were taking him deeper and deeper still.

"It will be soon," he said with one long, hard stroke. When she didn't speak but moaned, he added, "I told you I wanted forever." He held his breath, silently praying that she was on the same page as he was. He didn't think he could take it if she wasn't. He'd waited for her for over a year, and he didn't intend to wait any longer.

"That's a cheap proposal." Grabbing his bottom and cradling him inside her she opened her eyes as understanding of his last sentence registered.

"Yeah, well, I'll make it up to you later." Drifting into the passion that was their own, all conversation was forgotten. The only language spoken was strictly the language of lovers.

CHAPTER TWENTY-FOUR

First Baptist Church was packed to capacity on Sunday morning. They had been back in the city for a week, and Keith had reminded her of her invitation for him to go to church with her. She led him to a seat on the far side of the church away from where she normally sat, as they were a little late. Keith had brought breakfast, bagels and coffee, to her apartment earlier this morning, and Cienna had supplied the dessert.

So at twenty-after-eleven they were seated and listening to the choir sing. Cienna sang and clapped along with the rest of the congregation while Keith sat attentively watching his surroundings.

When it was time for the offering, Cienna retrieved her already prepared offering envelope and watched out of the corner of her eye as Keith placed a twenty-dollar bill in the chrome plate.

"How much do you put in?" he whispered.

"I tithe. That's ten percent of my weekly income." She watched as his eyes grew larger calculating the amount in his head. "Don't look at me like that," she whispered. You have no idea how much I make in a week." She laughed quietly.

"I know what I make, and that's comparison enough. And just why do you tithe?" he asked her seriously.

"It's my commitment to the Lord. He has blessed me with me the knowledge I needed to obtain the job that He set out for me to do, so the least I can do is give Him ten percent back."

He still didn't understand. He had lots of questions about this religion and church thing. But he planned to be with her for the rest of his life, so he knew he'd be coming to church more frequently. He'd ask his questions later. Right now, he just wanted to enjoy the steps they'd taken towards their future. He sat back in the pew and listened as the minister preached.

"So what did you think?" Cienna asked as they stood to leave the sanctuary.

"It was informative. I'll have to visit a few more times to have a real opinion."

"What did you feel? What did you feel in here as you listened to him talk?" Cienna placed her hand on his heart.

"There were moments when I felt like he was talking directly to me, and I guess that made me wonder a little." He spoke honestly as he placed his hand over hers. "Want to know what I'm feeling right now?" His eyes were clouded with ardor.

"Keep it to yourself because my mother's making her way to us."

"Damn!" Keith said quietly, closing his suit jacket so that Cienna's mother couldn't see the evidence of what her daughter did to him.

"Mornin', baby. I was afraid you weren't coming," Cienna's mother said, hugging her tightly.

"I was just a little late, Mama. I brought a friend with me. Keith Page, this is my mother, Adelle Turner. Mama, this is Keith Page. He's an associate at the firm," Cienna said, even though she figured her mother would remember him from their prior conversations.

"It's nice to finally meet you, ma'am." Keith held his hand out to Adelle.

Adelle Turner studied the man her daughter had called a friend, noting that this was the first 'friend' that Cienna had ever brought to church with her. This was also the first 'friend' to call her in a frantic search for her daughter. From the looks of them, he was quickly becoming more than a friend.

"It's a pleasure to meet you," Adelle said, swiping Keith's hand away and grabbing him against her for a hug. "God bless you," she said exuberantly.

"Ah, thank you," he said when she let him go. Cienna stood behind them smiling. Keith looked dazed and confused.

"So where're you two off to now?" Adelle asked.

"Ah, I'm going home, and Keith's going to play ball with his friends," Cienna answered.

"I cooked. Why don't you come on over and have dinner with your father and me?"

"Well…," Cienna hesitated.

"We'd love to come to your house for dinner," Keith interrupted, answering for them both.

"But I thought you were playing ball?" she said.

"I can play ball next Sunday." He gave her a wide grin.

"Good, then I'll see you both at the house. I gotta go see Sister Ruby for a second." Adelle reached over to hug her daughter again. "He sure is cute," she whispered in Cienna's ear.

"I guess you're coming to dinner," Cienna said when Adelle walked away.

"I guess I am, and maybe at dinner you'll introduce me as more than your 'friend.' "

Cienna chewed on her bottom lip. "Oh, you heard that, huh?"

"Yes, I heard it, and I understand why you were hesitant. But, baby, if we're going to be together, you've got to trust our feelings for each other. It's okay to tell people." With his arm around her, he pulled her closer as they walked to the car.

"I guess you're right," she reluctantly admitted.

They were eating in the dining room tonight. Company was there. An old oak table held all the Turner finery and boasted a homely scene for its guests. Adelle had laid out her best china, and the silverware sparkled after a fresh shining earlier this morning.

Keith and Cienna's father, Donald, sat in the living room discussing the ins and outs of golf. Ever since Tiger Woods hit the scene, every black man in America had begun to think they could play. Her father had been going to the driving range for about six months now. Every spare chance he got, he was there. And on the days that he was relieved from his duty at the post office early enough, he could usually be found out on the course perfecting his new game.

Cienna had had no idea that Keith was interested in golf; he'd only talked about basketball with her. But then she wasn't a man, and she didn't know much about either sport so it was probably best that he hadn't shared that with her.

She watched the two men that she held dearest in her heart sit in front of the television examining Tiger's stance and his swing. Her father must have taped one of the matches. It was a highly intellectual conversation for the avid sports addict, one that she chose wisely not to interrupt.

"They still at it?" Adelle asked when Cienna walked into the kitchen.

"Yeah. I don't know what they see in that sport. It's so boring." Leaning her butt against the counter, Cienna watched her mother make the gravy that would smother the pork chops that baked in the oven.

"I know it. And Donald has it on all the time. If he's not watching it, he's playing it. Works on my nerves." Carefully measuring the flour, Adelle waited for her daughter to tell her what was on her mind.

She had looked a lot more at peace when she walked in this evening with her man trailing behind her. Adelle thought that maybe she'd come to terms with the past and decided to move forward. Lord, how she hoped that was the case. Cienna had gone through so much in her young life; she just wished some happiness would come her way soon.

"You know, Mama, Keith's really nothing like Bobby."

"That's a good thing, right?"

"Yeah, I guess so." Cienna picked up the small knife and began to peel the potatoes that lay on the cutting board. "I don't think I ever felt this way with Bobby."

"Love's funny that way," Adelle added.

"Maybe I didn't love him at all."

"I think you did, as much as a twenty-three-year-old is capable of loving someone. You see, as you mature your capacity to love matures. And while you may have felt really strongly about Bobby and probably did love him in your own way at the time, your expectations are different now. You're different now. You understand what I'm saying?"

"I think so." Continuing to peel the potatoes, Cienna figured this was as good a time as any to tell her mother her news. "He wants to get married."

Minutes passed as she waited for Adelle's reaction to her announcement.

"Did you hear me, Mama?" When she heard nothing from her usually talkative mother, Cienna became concerned.

"I heard you." Adelle had heard her loud and clear. "Do you want to get married?"

"I don't know. I mean, I think I do one day." Thoughtfully, Cienna glanced at her mother. She was still a beautiful woman at fifty-six. With her hair styled and her nails manicured, Adelle looked just as at home in the kitchen as she had in the office. Cienna wondered if she'd be the same way. "What's it like to have it all, Mama?"

"It's like the biggest, best blessing you could ever imagine." Turning to her daughter, Adelle couldn't hide the tears that threatened to fall. "I want you to be happy. I haven't seen you truly happy in a long time. But this man has put a spark back in your eyes that I feared was long gone. God sent him to you for a reason. Now you be sure you don't throw away your blessings before you get the chance to truly experience them." Wiping her hands on her apron, Adelle took her daughter into her arms.

"I want a love like you and Daddy, Mama. Do you think I can have that?" Cienna asked, resting her chin on her mother's shoulder.

"You can have that and so much more, but you have to work hard and stay true to yourself. Let the Lord do the rest." Kissing her daughter on her forehead, Adelle stepped away. Dabbing at her eyes with the hem of her apron, she changed the subject.

"Now hurry up with those potatoes. We want to eat them with the rest of the meal," she admonished.

"I'm moving as fast as I can, Mama." Cienna returned to her chore.

"That ain't fast enough. Those men'll be hungry real soon, and I like to have the food ready when the stomach's ready. And watch what you're doing. You're puttin' all the meat in the trashcan with the peelings."

Cienna chuckled, to herself of course, and continued with the business she was about. She realized all of a sudden that she hated peeling potatoes. Always had and probably always would.

CHAPTER TWENTY-FIVE

Two Weeks Later

Benton and King and RES were in an uproar because of Mionne's suicide and the murder of Simms and Charles. The communications deal was awarded to another company, and stock in RES had plummeted. Benton and King had suffered from all the bad publicity involving Charles and Simms.

"I wonder what's going to happen now?" Reka was talking to Tacoma as he stood at the front desk with her.

"Hmph, I don't have a clue. The Board of Directors didn't look happy when they filed into the conference room."

"I guess we'd better get out the employment section."

"Girl, I've already started looking. Things don't look too good around here." Then Tacoma raised an elegantly arched eyebrow and said, "Can you believe all that about Mionne?"

"No, I can't. I mean she had a snippy little attitude sometimes, but who would have ever thought she was a cold-blooded murderer? And a freak to boot."

"I know, prostitution is so played out," Tacoma frowned.

"It's so nasty. What with AIDS and all those other disgusting STDs out there. You would think she had better sense than that." Reka paused only to answer the phone. Rolling her eyes, she disconnected.

"Who was that?" Tacoma asked.

"Another crank call. We should get the number changed."

"They're probably going to close down the firm anyway."

"I don't think they're going to do that. The firm still has a pretty heavy client base, and as long as Cienna and Keith don't bail out, the firm should still be in good shape," Reka surmised.

"Yeah, but they've got a lot of damage control to do."

"True."

Their conversation ceased as they heard footsteps approaching. The Board of Directors meeting was over, and several members came around the hall to stand near Reka's desk to wait for the elevator.

"I think it's a good plan," one man in a dark suit was saying.

A man Reka recognized as the Chairman of the Board spoke with a grim look on his face. "I guess it'll work. But we've got to keep a close eye on things from now on."

The elevator arrived, and the men boarded, both giving Reka a curt nod as the doors closed.

"I wonder what happened?" Tacoma whispered.

Byran King came down the hall with Cienna and Keith right behind him. "This is a good plan. Now let's see if you two can make it work. You're getting married, and I can't say that it'll be easy for husband and wife to work together."

Cienna smiled in response. "I think we're managing so far to separate our professional lives from the personal ones pretty well, considering everything that's happened," she said as they approached the elevators.

Keith put a protective arm around her. He'd seen the small glimmer of embarrassment shadow her eyes when Byran commented on their personal life. He knew that she still had trouble combining their two worlds, but she was making a valiant effort, and for that he was supremely grateful. In the past couple of weeks they'd grown closer as their relationship had been thrust into the public eye.

Cienna had been surprisingly strong. He'd watched her carefully, waiting for her to fall apart. But she never did. She'd answered the police's extensive questioning, and she had handled the press with ease and finesse. He was proud of her. And each time she stood beside him smiling, whether it be in the capacity of an attorney or her newfound position as his fiancée, she'd done so in a fashion so regal, so professional, so admirable that his heart swelled with immense love for her.

"I think our personal feelings will enhance the rebirth of the firm. Not only are we committed to each other, we are committed to rebuilding the good name and impeccable character of the firm that Charles Benton stained." Keith's gaze swept over Cienna and landed on Byran.

"I'm sure you'll do a fine job. Both of you are excellent attorneys, and with everything you've been through, I'm sure you've become stronger people in the process. I'm going to keep my eye on you, but not because I think you'll fail. I'm anxious to see the good work I know is in store for the firm." Byran spoke enthusiastically. "That sexual harassment policy you proposed is an excellent idea. I'm glad you'll be leading the effort," he said to Cienna.

"I agree. We should do a little more research on getting the right risk manager to come in and evaluate the plan but otherwise I think it's a good start," Keith said.

"I'm glad we all agree. As attorneys who defend the employers in these matters—we should set the example," Cienna added emphatically.

"You're absolutely right. And we will set the example, a damn good example at that." Byran thrust his hand forward toward her.

Cienna smiled, extending her own hand. "Thank you, Byran."

Keith extended his hand and shook Byran's heartily. "You won't be disappointed, Byran. I can guarantee that."

The elevator bell chimed, and Byran walked away with a smile and a wave to Tacoma and Reka, who had been eagerly listening to his conversation with Cienna and Keith. "Good day."

"Have a good day, Mr. King." Reka smiled and waved in return. Tacoma repeated her actions.

"So what's up?" Reka asked as soon as the elevator doors closed.

"Yeah, do we sink or swim?" Tacoma chimed in.

Cienna and Keith moved closer to the front desk. "It was unbelievable, the meeting, I mean," Cienna said. "Most of the partners were all for dissolving the business, afraid of all the damage done by the scandal. But then there were a few,"

"The most important few," Keith interrupted.

Cienna smiled in his direction. "Yeah, the big cheeses that supported the idea that Keith and I came up with."

"And what idea was that?" Reka asked.

"Reka, I'm shocked." Cienna feigned surprise.

"What?" Reka's eyes widened.

"There's something going on around here that you don't know about?" Cienna laughed at Reka's befuddled look.

"I know, I've been trying to tell her she's been slipping lately. There's been just too much drama that we didn't have firsthand knowledge about. I'm a little distressed myself." Tacoma lifted his hand to his chest in astonishment.

Keith chuckled. "Cienna and I have decided to take over the firm. While we don't have controlling stock, we've been made full-fledged partners. Cienna will be the managing partner overseeing hiring, firing, firm policies and personnel. I'll be acting as supervising partner handling marketing, recruiting, advertising, things like that. We're going to be pretty busy around here in the coming months. We've got to rebuild."

"Oh, my God. That's a pretty big deal." Tacoma was surprised.

"Damn, you're moving up in the world, huh?" Reka looked at Cienna.

"It's about damn time!" Cienna exclaimed. "The wedding's in March." To add icing to the cake, she thrust her hand over the desk into Reka's line of vision. She wiggled her fingers, and the fluorescent lighting bounced off the four-karat diamond on her ring finger.

"Daaaaaaammmmnnn! Put that thing away before I go blind!" Tacoma shielded his eyes.

Reka grabbed Cienna's hand, tilting it from side to side. "It's all right, I guess." She sucked her teeth. "Is this the best you could do, Casanova?" Her eyes fell on Keith.

"She's not complaining," he defended.

"Yeah, well, I'll be monitoring your phone calls from now on," Reka told him.

"As if you haven't been monitoring them in the past." Keith smiled, remembering the calls from Tyra. Tyra hadn't called since the scandal hit the public, the one good thing to come of this whole mess. He'd been afraid he'd have a harassment case himself dealing with her and her incessant phone calls. Thankfully, she'd come to her senses and decided he wasn't worth it.

The foursome laughed, all of them relieved that things were on the road to normal, though they were still shocked and saddened by the actions of people they had known and respected.

"All I want to know now is…do I still have a job?" Reka asked seriously. "'Cause a sister needs to find a new apartment. Jeff is history. I put his lying ass out, but he still has a key so I need to relocate."

Tacoma rolled his eyes. Cienna hid a grin. Keith laughed openly.

"Yeah, you still have a job, but I don't want any of those sorry-ass men you date calling here all day long. You're going to become an Administrative Assistant. We're going to pay for you to take some classes at the community college, and your duties are going to increase around here. It's time to stop wasting your life," Cienna informed her. She had thought about this last night. Reka had a lot of potential, and she felt compelled to help her. She hadn't been able to help Mionne. She hadn't tried hard enough. In time, she'd deal with everything Mionne had said to her the night of her death. And she was going to start by changing things for the better both in her life and in the lives of others.

EPILOGUE

Two years later.

"We're going to be late," Keith announced as he watched Cienna slip into a pair of black Italian pumps. He wondered how in the hell she could walk on those stilts. But she did it, and she did it well, too.

"I'm moving as fast as I can. I can't help that I was momentarily detained." Twenty minutes ago, she had been pinned against the wall of the shower while Keith pounded into her in deep concentration.

"Yeah? I didn't hear you complaining then," he smirked.

"And I'm not complaining now," she smiled. "We have to get it when we can," she said just as Tianna let out a squeal.

"I know that's right! I sure will be glad when she gets her days and nights together," Keith said.

"Baby, you're horny day and night, so I don't think it really matters when she wakes up." Cienna left the room to retrieve her crying child.

"Come on, princess, tonight is Daddy's big night. Now that I've already taken care of part of his victory celebration, it's time for us to get started on the other part," she was saying as Keith came out of the bedroom.

"Don't tell her that. She'll think nasty thoughts."

"Her father's nasty, and her mother can hold her own, so you know what they say."

Keith laughed as she walked past him and grabbed his crotch. "Come on and stop playing. We have to be there by eight."

"We'll be there."

"We're going to be late," he was muttering as they started down the street. "It's not going to look good, the newest District Court Judge late for his swearing in."

"It's not going to look good if we arrive in a body bag either," Cienna said, commenting on the way he had screeched out of the driveway.

"I'm just excited, you know, like you were when King begged you to be a full partner." Out of the corner of his eye, he admired the woman who sat in the seat across from him. She had come such a long way. Work was no longer the priority. Though she was damn good at it, she knew how to walk away from it when it was necessary.

"I know. I'm excited too." She patted his hand. "Things are going smoothly for both of us. All of us."

She motioned towards their daughter who lay quietly in her car seat.

Halfway to the courthouse, Keith stopped the car to stare at his wife. A quick glance in the backseat confirmed that his daughter was fast asleep in her car seat. "Feel like a quickie?" Grinning, he waited for her response.

"Don't you ever get enough?" she exclaimed.

"Nope." He leaned over to kiss her waiting mouth. "Never."

2009 Reprint Mass Market Titles

January

I'm Gonna Make You Love Me
Gweneth Bolton
ISBN-13: 978-1-58571-294-6
$6.99

Shades of Desire
Monica White
ISBN-13: 978-1-58571-292-2
$6.99

February

A Love of Her Own
Cheris Hodges
ISBN-13: 978-1-58571-293-9
$6.99

Color of Trouble
Dyanne Davis
ISBN-13: 978-1-58571-294-6
$6.99

March

Twist of Fate
Beverly Clark
ISBN-13: 978-1-58571-295-3
$6.99

Chances
Pamela Leigh Starr
ISBN-13: 978-1-58571-296-0
$6.99

April

Sinful Intentions
Crystal Rhodes
ISBN-13: 978-1-585712-297-7
$6.99

Rock Star
Roslyn Hardy Holcomb
ISBN-13: 978-1-58571-298-4
$6.99

May

Paths of Fire
T.T. Henderson
ISBN-13: 978-1-58571-343-1
$6.99

Caugth Up in the Rapture
Lisa Riley
ISBN-13: 978-1-58571-344-8
$6.99

June

Reckless Surrender
Rochelle Alers
ISBN-13: 978-1-58571-345-5
$6.99

No Ordinary Love
Angela Weaver
ISBN-13: 978-1-58571-346-2
$6.99

2009 Reprint Mass Market Titles (continued)

July

Intentional Mistakes
Michele Sudler
ISBN-13: 978-1-58571-347-9
$6.99

It's In His Kiss
Reon Carter
ISBN-13: 978-1-58571-348-6
$6.99

August

Unfinished Love Affair
Barbara Keaton
ISBN-13: 978-1-58571-349-3
$6.99

A Perfect Place to Pray
I.L Goodwin
ISBN-13: 978-1-58571-299-1
$6.99

September

Love in High Gear
Charlotte Roy
ISBN-13: 978-1-58571-355-4
$6.99

Ebony Eyes
Kei Swanson
ISBN-13: 978-1-58571-356-1
$6.99

October

Midnight Clear, Part I
Leslie Esdale/Carmen Green
ISBN-13: 978-1-58571-357-8
$6.99

Midnight Clear, Part II
Gwynne Forster/Monica
     Jackson
ISBN-13: 978-1-58571-358-5
$6.99

November

Midnight Peril
Vicki Andrews
ISBN-13: 978-1-58571-359-2
$6.99

One Day At A Time
Bella McFarland
ISBN-13: 978-1-58571-360-8
$6.99

December

Just An Affair
Eugenia O'Neal
ISBN-13: 978-1-58571-361-5
$6.99

Shades of Brown
Denise Becker
ISBN-13: 978-1-58571-362-2
$6.99

2009 New Mass Market Titles

January

Singing A Song...
Crystal Rhodes
ISBN-13: 978-1-58571-283-0
$6.99

Look Both Ways
Joan Early
ISBN-13: 978-1-58571-284-7
$6.99

February

Six O'Clock
Katrina Spencer
ISBN-13: 978-1-58571-285-4
$6.99

Red Sky
Renee Alexis
ISBN-13: 978-1-58571-286-1
$6.99

March

Anything But Love
Celya Bowers
ISBN-13: 978-1-58571-287-8
$6.99

Tempting Faith
Crystal Hubbard
ISBN-13: 978-1-58571-288-5
$6.99

April

If I Were Your Woman
La Connie Taylor-Jones
ISBN-13: 978-1-58571-289-2
$6.99

Best Of Luck Elsewhere
Trisha Haddad
ISBN-13: 978-1-58571-290-8
$6.99

May

All I'll Ever Need
Mildred Riley
ISBN-13: 978-1-58571-335-6
$6.99

A Place Like Home
Alicia Wiggins
ISBN-13: 978-1-58571-336-3
$6.99

June

Best Foot Forward
Michele Sudler
ISBN-13: 978-1-58571-337-0
$6.99

It's In the Rhythm
Sammie Ward
ISBN-13: 978-1-58571-338-7
$6.99

2009 New Mass Market Titles (continued)

July

Checks and Balances
Elaine Sims
ISBN-13: 978-1-58571-339-4
$6.99

Save Me
Africa Fine
ISBN-13: 978-1-58571-340-0
$6.99

August

When Lightening Strikes
Michele Cameron
ISBN-13: 978-1-58571-369-1
$6.99

Blindsided
Tammy Williams
ISBN-13: 978-1-58571-342-4
$6.99

September

2 Good
Celya Bowers
ISBN-13: 978-1-58571-350-9
$6.99

Waiting for Mr. Darcy
Chamein Canton
ISBN-13: 978-1-58571-351-6
$6.99

October

Fireflies
Joan Early
ISBN-13: 978-1-58571-352-3
$6.99

Frost On My Window
Angela Weaver
ISBN-13: 978-1-58571-353-0
$6.99

November

Waiting in the Shadows
Michele Sudler
ISBN-13: 978-1-58571-364-6
$6.99

Fixin' Tyrone
Keith Walker
ISBN-13: 978-1-58571-365-3
$6.99

December

Dream Keeper
Gail McFarland
ISBN-13: 978-1-58571-366-0
$6.99

Another Memory
Pamela Ridley
ISBN-13: 978-1-58571-367-7
$6.99

Other Genesis Press, Inc. Titles

Other Genesis Press, Inc. Titles (continued)

Bodyguard	Andrea Jackson	$9.95
Boss of Me	Diana Nyad	$8.95
Bound by Love	Beverly Clark	$8.95
Breeze	Robin Hampton Allen	$10.95
Broken	Dar Tomlinson	$24.95
By Design	Barbara Keaton	$8.95
Cajun Heat	Charlene Berry	$8.95
Careless Whispers	Rochelle Alers	$8.95
Cats & Other Tales	Marilyn Wagner	$8.95
Caught in a Trap	Andre Michelle	$8.95
Caught Up In the Rapture	Lisa G. Riley	$9.95
Cautious Heart	Cheris F Hodges	$8.95
Chances	Pamela Leigh Starr	$8.95
Cherish the Flame	Beverly Clark	$8.95
Choices	Tammy Williams	$6.99
Class Reunion	Irma Jenkins/ John Brown	$12.95
Code Name: Diva	J.M. Jeffries	$9.95
Conquering Dr. Wexler's Heart	Kimberley White	$9.95
Corporate Seduction	A.C. Arthur	$9.95
Crossing Paths, Tempting Memories	Dorothy Elizabeth Love	$9.95
Crush	Crystal Hubbard	$9.95
Cypress Whisperings	Phyllis Hamilton	$8.95
Dark Embrace	Crystal Wilson Harris	$8.95
Dark Storm Rising	Chinelu Moore	$10.95
Daughter of the Wind	Joan Xian	$8.95
Dawn's Harbor	Kymberly Hunt	$6.99
Deadly Sacrifice	Jack Kean	$22.95
Designer Passion	Dar Tomlinson Diana Richeaux	$8.95
Do Over	Celya Bowers	$9.95
Dream Runner	Gail McFarland	$6.99
Dreamtective	Liz Swados	$5.95

Other Genesis Press, Inc. Titles (continued)

Ebony Angel	Deatri King-Bey	$9.95
Ebony Butterfly II	Delilah Dawson	$14.95
Echoes of Yesterday	Beverly Clark	$9.95
Eden's Garden	Elizabeth Rose	$8.95
Eve's Prescription	Edwina Martin Arnold	$8.95
Everlastin' Love	Gay G. Gunn	$8.95
Everlasting Moments	Dorothy Elizabeth Love	$8.95
Everything and More	Sinclair Lebeau	$8.95
Everything but Love	Natalie Dunbar	$8.95
Falling	Natalie Dunbar	$9.95
Fate	Pamela Leigh Starr	$8.95
Finding Isabella	A.J. Garrotto	$8.95
Forbidden Quest	Dar Tomlinson	$10.95
Forever Love	Wanda Y. Thomas	$8.95
From the Ashes	Kathleen Suzanne	$8.95
	Jeanne Sumerix	
Gentle Yearning	Rochelle Alers	$10.95
Glory of Love	Sinclair LeBeau	$10.95
Go Gentle into that	Malcom Boyd	$12.95
Good Night		
Goldengroove	Mary Beth Craft	$16.95
Groove, Bang, and Jive	Steve Cannon	$8.99
Hand in Glove	Andrea Jackson	$9.95
Hard to Love	Kimberley White	$9.95
Hart & Soul	Angie Daniels	$8.95
Heart of the Phoenix	A.C. Arthur	$9.95
Heartbeat	Stephanie Bedwell-Grime	$8.95
Hearts Remember	M. Loui Quezada	$8.95
Hidden Memories	Robin Allen	$10.95
Higher Ground	Leah Latimer	$19.95
Hitler, the War, and the Pope	Ronald Rychlak	$26.95
How to Write a Romance	Kathryn Falk	$18.95
I Married a Reclining Chair	Lisa M. Fuhs	$8.95
I'll Be Your Shelter	Giselle Carmichael	$8.95
I'll Paint a Sun	A.J. Garrotto	$9.95

Other Genesis Press, Inc. Titles (continued)

Icie	Pamela Leigh Starr	$8.95
Illusions	Pamela Leigh Starr	$8.95
Indigo After Dark Vol. I	Nia Dixon/Angelique	$10.95
Indigo After Dark Vol. II	Dolores Bundy/ Cole Riley	$10.95
Indigo After Dark Vol. III	Montana Blue/ Coco Morena	$10.95
Indigo After Dark Vol. IV	Cassandra Colt/	$14.95
Indigo After Dark Vol. V	Delilah Dawson	$14.95
Indiscretions	Donna Hill	$8.95
Intentional Mistakes	Michele Sudler	$9.95
Interlude	Donna Hill	$8.95
Intimate Intentions	Angie Daniels	$8.95
It's Not Over Yet	J.J. Michael	$9.95
Jolie's Surrender	Edwina Martin-Arnold	$8.95
Kiss or Keep	Debra Phillips	$8.95
Lace	Giselle Carmichael	$9.95
Lady Preacher	K.T. Richey	$6.99
Last Train to Memphis	Elsa Cook	$12.95
Lasting Valor	Ken Olsen	$24.95
Let Us Prey	Hunter Lundy	$25.95
Lies Too Long	Pamela Ridley	$13.95
Life Is Never As It Seems	J.J. Michael	$12.95
Lighter Shade of Brown	Vicki Andrews	$8.95
Looking for Lily	Africa Fine	$6.99
Love Always	Mildred E. Riley	$10.95
Love Doesn't Come Easy	Charlyne Dickerson	$8.95
Love Unveiled	Gloria Greene	$10.95
Love's Deception	Charlene Berry	$10.95
Love's Destiny	M. Loui Quezada	$8.95
Love's Secrets	Yolanda McVey	$6.99
Mae's Promise	Melody Walcott	$8.95
Magnolia Sunset	Giselle Carmichael	$8.95 .
Many Shades of Gray	Dyanne Davis	$6.99
Matters of Life and Death	Lesego Malepe, Ph.D.	$15.95

Other Genesis Press, Inc. Titles (continued)

Meant to Be	Jeanne Sumerix	$8.95
Midnight Clear	Leslie Esdaile	$10.95
(Anthology)	Gwynne Forster	
	Carmen Green	
	Monica Jackson	
Midnight Magic	Gwynne Forster	$8.95
Midnight Peril	Vicki Andrews	$10.95
Misconceptions	Pamela Leigh Starr	$9.95
Moments of Clarity	Michele Cameron	$6.99
Montgomery's Children	Richard Perry	$14.95
Mr Fix-It	Crystal Hubbard	$6.99
My Buffalo Soldier	Barbara B. K. Reeves	$8.95
Naked Soul	Gwynne Forster	$8.95
Never Say Never	Michele Cameron	$6.99
Next to Last Chance	Louisa Dixon	$24.95
No Apologies	Seressia Glass	$8.95
No Commitment Required	Seressia Glass	$8.95
No Regrets	Mildred E. Riley	$8.95
Not His Type	Chamein Canton	$6.99
Nowhere to Run	Gay G. Gunn	$10.95
O Bed! O Breakfast!	Rob Kuehnle	$14.95
Object of His Desire	A. C. Arthur	$8.95
Office Policy	A. C. Arthur	$9.95
Once in a Blue Moon	Dorianne Cole	$9.95
One Day at a Time	Bella McFarland	$8.95
One in A Million	Barbara Keaton	$6.99
One of These Days	Michele Sudler	$9.95
Outside Chance	Louisa Dixon	$24.95
Passion	T.T. Henderson	$10.95
Passion's Blood	Cherif Fortin	$22.95
Passion's Furies	AlTonya Washington	$6.99
Passion's Journey	Wanda Y. Thomas	$8.95
Past Promises	Jahmel West	$8.95
Path of Fire	T.T. Henderson	$8.95
Path of Thorns	Annetta P. Lee	$9.95

Other Genesis Press, Inc. Titles (continued)

Peace Be Still	Colette Haywood	$12.95
Picture Perfect	Reon Carter	$8.95
Playing for Keeps	Stephanie Salinas	$8.95
Pride & Joi	Gay G. Gunn	$8.95
Promises Made	Bernice Layton	$6.99
Promises to Keep	Alicia Wiggins	$8.95
Quiet Storm	Donna Hill	$10.95
Reckless Surrender	Rochelle Alers	$6.95
Red Polka Dot in a World of Plaid	Varian Johnson	$12.95
Reluctant Captive	Joyce Jackson	$8.95
Rendezvous with Fate	Jeanne Sumerix	$8.95
Revelations	Cheris F. Hodges	$8.95
Rivers of the Soul	Leslie Esdaile	$8.95
Rocky Mountain Romance	Kathleen Suzanne	$8.95
Rooms of the Heart	Donna Hill	$8.95
Rough on Rats and Tough on Cats	Chris Parker	$12.95
Secret Library Vol. 1	Nina Sheridan	$18.95
Secret Library Vol. 2	Cassandra Colt	$8.95
Secret Thunder	Annetta P. Lee	$9.95
Shades of Brown	Denise Becker	$8.95
Shades of Desire	Monica White	$8.95
Shadows in the Moonlight	Jeanne Sumerix	$8.95
Sin	Crystal Rhodes	$8.95
Small Whispers	Annetta P. Lee	$6.99
So Amazing	Sinclair LeBeau	$8.95
Somebody's Someone	Sinclair LeBeau	$8.95
Someone to Love	Alicia Wiggins	$8.95
Song in the Park	Martin Brant	$15.95
Soul Eyes	Wayne L. Wilson	$12.95
Soul to Soul	Donna Hill	$8.95
Southern Comfort	J.M. Jeffries	$8.95
Southern Fried Standards	S.R. Maddox	$6.99
Still the Storm	Sharon Robinson	$8.95

Other Genesis Press, Inc. Titles (continued)

Still Waters Run Deep	Leslie Esdaile	$8.95
Stolen Kisses	Dominiqua Douglas	$9.95
Stolen Memories	Michele Sudler	$6.99
Stories to Excite You	Anna Forrest/Divine	$14.95
Storm	Pamela Leigh Starr	$6.99
Subtle Secrets	Wanda Y. Thomas	$8.95
Suddenly You	Crystal Hubbard	$9.95
Sweet Repercussions	Kimberley White	$9.95
Sweet Sensations	Gwendolyn Bolton	$9.95
Sweet Tomorrows	Kimberly White	$8.95
Taken by You	Dorothy Elizabeth Love	$9.95
Tattooed Tears	T. T. Henderson	$8.95
The Color Line	Lizzette Grayson Carter	$9.95
The Color of Trouble	Dyanne Davis	$8.95
The Disappearance of Allison Jones	Kayla Perrin	$5.95
The Fires Within	Beverly Clark	$9.95
The Foursome	Celya Bowers	$6.99
The Honey Dipper's Legacy	Pannell-Allen	$14.95
The Joker's Love Tune	Sidney Rickman	$15.95
The Little Pretender	Barbara Cartland	$10.95
The Love We Had	Natalie Dunbar	$8.95
The Man Who Could Fly	Bob & Milana Beamon	$18.95
The Missing Link	Charlyne Dickerson	$8.95
The Mission	Pamela Leigh Starr	$6.99
The More Things Change	Chamein Canton	$6.99
The Perfect Frame	Beverly Clark	$9.95
The Price of Love	Sinclair LeBeau	$8.95
The Smoking Life	Ilene Barth	$29.95
The Words of the Pitcher	Kei Swanson	$8.95
Things Forbidden	Maryam Diaab	$6.99
This Life Isn't Perfect Holla	Sandra Foy	$6.99
Three Doors Down	Michele Sudler	$6.99
Three Wishes	Seressia Glass	$8.95
Ties That Bind	Kathleen Suzanne	$8.95

Other Genesis Press, Inc. Titles (continued)

Tiger Woods	Libby Hughes	$5.95
Time is of the Essence	Angie Daniels	$9.95
Timeless Devotion	Bella McFarland	$9.95
Tomorrow's Promise	Leslie Esdaile	$8.95
Truly Inseparable	Wanda Y. Thomas	$8.95
Two Sides to Every Story	Dyanne Davis	$9.95
Unbreak My Heart	Dar Tomlinson	$8.95
Uncommon Prayer	Kenneth Swanson	$9.95
Unconditional Love	Alicia Wiggins	$8.95
Unconditional	A.C. Arthur	$9.95
Undying Love	Renee Alexis	$6.99
Until Death Do Us Part	Susan Paul	$8.95
Vows of Passion	Bella McFarland	$9.95
Wedding Gown	Dyanne Davis	$8.95
What's Under Benjamin's Bed	Sandra Schaffer	$8.95
When A Man Loves A Woman	La Connie Taylor-Jones	$6.99
When Dreams Float	Dorothy Elizabeth Love	$8.95
When I'm With You	LaConnie Taylor-Jones	$6.99
Where I Want To Be	Maryam Diaab	$6.99
Whispers in the Night	Dorothy Elizabeth Love	$8.95
Whispers in the Sand	LaFlorya Gauthier	$10.95
Who's That Lady?	Andrea Jackson	$9.95
Wild Ravens	Altonya Washington	$9.95
Yesterday Is Gone	Beverly Clark	$10.95
Yesterday's Dreams, Tomorrow's Promises	Reon Laudat	$8.95
Your Precious Love	Sinclair LeBeau	$8.95

Dull, Drab, Love Life?

Passion Going Nowhere?

Tired Of Being Alone?

Does Every Direction You Look For Love

Lead You Astray?

Genesis Press presents
The launching of our new website!

RecaptureTheRomance.Com

Ignite
The Flame!

ESCAPE WITH INDIGO !!!!

Join Indigo Book Club©
It's simple, easy and secure.

Sign up and receive the new
releases
every month + Free shipping
and
20% off the cover price.

Go online to www.genesis-
press.com and click on Bookclub
or
call 1-888-INDIGO-1

Order Form

Mail to: Genesis Press, Inc.
P.O. Box 101
Columbus, MS 39703

Name _____
Address _____
City/State _____ Zip _____
Telephone _____

Ship to (if different from above)
Name _____
Address _____
City/State _____ Zip _____
Telephone _____

Credit Card Information
Credit Card # _____ ☐ Visa ☐ Mastercard
Expiration Date (mm/yy) _____ ☐ AmEx ☐ Discover

Qty.	Author	Title	Price	Total

Use this order form, or call 1-888-INDIGO-1

Total for books	_____
Shipping and handling: $5 first two books, $1 each additional book	_____
Total S & H	_____
Total amount enclosed	_____

Mississippi residents add 7% sales tax